Family Night

ON

Union Station

EarthCent Ambassador Series:

Date Night on Union Station

Alien Night on Union Station

High Priest on Union Station

Spy Night on Union Station

Carnival on Union Station

Wanderers on Union Station

Vacation on Union Station

Guest Night on Union Station

Word Night on Union Station

Party Night on Union Station

Review Night on Union Station

Family Night on Union Station

Book Night on Union Station

LARP Night on Union Station

Book Twelve of EarthCent Ambassador

Family Night on Union Station

Foner Books

ISBN 978-1-948691-01-7

Copyright 2017 by E. M. Foner

Northampton, Massachusetts

In memory of my father, Mitchell. He introduced me to Victorian literature, 1930's madcap comedies, and taught me to appreciate happy endings.

One

"In conclusion, it is the view of Union Station Embassy that bedtime should be when we get sleepy."

"My turn, Fenna. That was your third one in a row."

"But my conclusions are much shorter than yours," the eight-year-old girl protested. She hung onto the edge of the ambassador's display desk as Mike tried to pull the chair away. "Tell them, Libby."

"I agree with your report to EarthCent one hundred percent," the Stryx librarian said. "I've analyzed the feedback from over forty billion InstaSitter assignments around the tunnel network stations, and an arbitrary bedtime is the primary cause of friction between sitters and clients across a broad range of species."

"You sent Fenna's report to EarthCent?" Mike asked in horror. "But we're just playing 'bassador."

Fenna pushed off with both of her hands and kept the chair moving with her feet, as if she had suddenly discovered that the display desk was on fire. "Did you really send my report, Libby? Grandma Kelly is going to be so mad."

"I didn't send it in the ambassador's name," the Stryx reassured her. "I signed it, 'Young Sentients Committee of Union Station.'"

1

"You can go next, Spinner," Mike offered, the attraction of playing at the ambassador's desk having suddenly lost its allure. If he had learned one thing from his father, who had recently promoted himself to Associate Ambassador, it was how committee work inevitably expanded to the point that there was no time left for playing.

Spinner floated up to the display desk and did a few half rotations from side to side before commencing.

"In conclusion, it is the view of Union Station Embassy that Stryx students in the station librarian's experimental school should not be coerced into studying multiverse mathematics while the biological children are sleeping, and I further request that the EarthCent president file an official discrimination complaint with the station management on the behalf of said victims."

"Where did you learn all those big words?" Mike demanded.

"Reading," the young Stryx replied modestly.

"Did you send that one too, Libby?" Fenna asked.

"Directly to Spinner's parent," the station librarian replied. "I imagine he's heard back already."

The young Stryx sank to the floor, rolled into the corner on his treads, and began reciting, "I will stop complaining about multiverse math homework," over and over again.

The door slid open and Kelly entered her office, blinking in surprise at finding the youngsters.

"Hey guys, what's up? Why is Spinner standing in the corner talking to himself?"

"Libby told on him to his parent," Mike said indignantly.

"And why is my chair so far from the desk?"

"We didn't want to accidentally send any messages to EarthCent or anything," the boy fibbed, shaking his head

2

at Fenna to keep her from confessing. "Is my dad's door open yet? He was supposed to take us to Libbyland, but he said he needed to stop in for a holo-thingy."

"I thought your mother was training the dog to keep your dad away from the embassy on weekends."

"She did, except Queenie won't leave the apartment when my mom is home alone with my little sister. Aunt Brinda says that the female Cayl hounds like to keep an eye on the youngest member of the pack."

"Well, I'm still the alpha ambassador around here, so let's go get your father out of that meeting. And Libby, I'd like to make an official EarthCent request on behalf of Spinner that you grant him a pardon for his latest transgression."

"I've relayed your communication, but that's up to his parent," the Stryx librarian responded.

"Thank you, Ambassador," Spinner said a moment later. He rose into the air and knocked out a number of rapid rotations to celebrate his reprieve from being grounded.

Kelly led the three youngsters out of her office and to the left. Then she almost punched Daniel in the nose by attempting to rap assertively on his door just as it slid open.

"Close call," the freshly-minted associate ambassador remarked. "It didn't occur to me that somebody might be assaulting my door when I recalibrated the proximity trigger."

"Why would you want the door to delay opening until you're practically hitting it with your face?"

"I like to move around the office during holo conferences, and I got fed up with triggering the door opener by mistake. My office isn't as large as yours, you know."

3

"I guess that explains why you let the children in to play at my desk," Kelly shot back. "I wondered how they got past the security."

"Spinner opened the door for us," Fenna confessed. "He's really good with locks and stuff."

"Sorry if the kids were bothering you," Daniel said. "I thought I'd be off the conference call in a jiffy, but you know how that goes. Hey, why are you here on a weekend?"

"I don't know, but I'll find out in seven minutes," Kelly replied after consulting her ornamental wristwatch. "I heard that you're all going to Libbyland."

"I promised to take Mike and Fenna on the Physics Ride now that they're old enough. Spinner is coming along to give them flying pointers."

"But no spinning," the girl added.

"Have a good time, then," Kelly said. "I'll ping you, Daniel, if my conference call turns out to be critical to the fate of the galaxy."

The ambassador and her associate shared a quick laugh over the well-worn EarthCent joke, and then the flying party set off, leaving Kelly alone in the embassy. She reentered her office, made a swiping gesture to lock the door, and pushed her chair back over to the display desk before taking her seat.

"What's this all about, Libby? I don't remember the last time the president called an emergency intelligence steering committee meeting."

"I hope you're using that as an expression and not because you're forgetting things," the Stryx librarian replied in a concerned voice. "And it wouldn't be appropriate for me to steal the president's thunder, especially when the conference is beginning in less than four minutes."

4

"Just a hint," Kelly pleaded. "Give me the first letter."

"A."

"Anarchy? Audit? Alarm?"

"Those all do begin with 'A,' but if I were a psychologist, I might infer a preoccupation with disaster on your part," Libby observed.

"Attack? Asteroid? Apocalypse?" Kelly continued undaunted. She closed her eyes and racked her brain for more candidates. "Abduction? Accursed? Avalanche?"

"Avalanche?" the president repeated in an amused tone.

Kelly's eyes snapped open and she saw a holographic projection of the president sitting across from her. "I just assumed it was something bad," she admitted. "Where are the other ambassadors?"

"They'll be with us in a minute. I wanted to talk to you first so you don't look surprised in front of the others, since you are our Minister of Intelligence. To be brief, an unidentified alien craft jumped into our solar system this evening. It jumped out again so quickly that we might have missed it, but the captain of a Dollnick cargo carrier waiting to dock at the space elevator hub sent us their assessment. The AI controlling our tunnel entrance for the Stryx confirmed the report."

"So it could have been some rich kids from any of the tunnel network species fooling around. What's the big deal?"

"We're confident it was a first contact situation, even though they left without saying anything. The other ambassadors will be coming on in a few seconds, and we'll be joined by Hep, who will explain further."

Holograms of the other steering committee members began popping into existence around Kelly's display desk, with several of the ambassadors nursing take-out cups of

5

steaming coffee. The president waited a minute for everybody to exchange greetings, and then repeated what he had already told the Union Station ambassador.

"So what do the Stryx have to say about all of this?" Ambassador Oshi inquired.

"Let's hear from our faster-than-light drive expert first, and then we'll get into that," President Beyer responded, and beckoned to an unseen figure. "Hep?"

The Verlock academy-trained mathematician stepped into the president's hologram and looked around at the steering committee ambassadors. "Real time holographic conferencing," he commented. "Stryxnet bandwidth must cost a fortune."

"EarthCent Intelligence covers the bill for our steering committee meetings," the president informed him. "They run at a small profit."

"As long as it's not coming out of my budget," Hep said agreeably. "Let me begin by saying that I don't want to waste any more of your time or my time than I have to. Although we have yet to come up with a theoretical explanation for basic jump drives that fits within the framework of humanity's current model of how the universe operates, our ongoing restoration contract for the earliest successful Drazen jump ship has allowed us to reverse engineer a mathematical simulation for testing new hypotheses."

"English, please," President Beyer interjected.

The scientist shot the president a sour look and continued. "One interesting observation is that even the crudest jump drives can be configured in an infinite variety of geometries, making the resulting usage signatures unique."

"You mean they leave fingerprints?" Ambassador White asked.

"Roughly speaking. Although the Dollnicks wouldn't normally share telemetry data with us for competitive reasons, the captain of the cargo carrier who initially spotted the jump was nice enough to alert EarthCent that the drive signature didn't match anything in their records. The tunnel master confirmed the Dollnick's assessment and sent us the actual data, which was really quite exciting in…"

"So we know whoever jumped into the solar system was using a jump drive configuration which even the Stryx haven't seen before," the president interrupted.

"Yes, and that's been the case every time that a new species independently develops their own faster-than-light drive," Hep replied. Then he added, "We could probably construct a working drive of our own at this point, but the signature would closely match that of a Drazen jump ship from around a half a million years ago."

"How is it that there are so many answers to the same question?" Ambassador Enoksen asked. "I could understand there being a number of different ways to solve a problem, but an infinite set of solutions?"

"Think of a jump drive as a bridge," Hep urged the diplomats. "Engineers around the galaxy who are tasked with spanning a wide river face the same basic challenge. But even if they were all utilizing an identical system of mathematics, their solutions would be influenced by the choice of local materials, the history of construction on their world, even aesthetics. Light years of distance represent a very wide river, and even small differences in design choices will leave their mark on the fabric of the space-time continuum. That is the signature."

"Clear as mud?" the president inquired of the ambassadors cheerfully. "Good. Thank you for stopping in, Hep. I won't keep you from your work any longer." The scientist gave the ambassadors a brief nod and exited the hologram.

"So we know that a new species has developed faster-than-light drive, but that must happen pretty regularly," Kelly pointed out.

"In geologic time, I'm sure it does, but consider how long life on Earth has bumbled along without creating our own jump technology," Ambassador Fu observed. "And now that I think of it, what are the odds that a species just reaching that level would put in their first appearance at our homeworld?"

"An event that carries with it a certain responsibility on our part," the president informed the others. "I've been notified by the Stryx that as the first point of contact for this as-of-yet unnamed species, humanity, or more particularly, EarthCent, has a contractual obligation to the tunnel network to lead the biological contingent in the welcoming mission."

"The Stryx welcoming mission?" Svetlana asked.

"Exactly. Transportation will be provided by one of their science ships, which I'm sure you all know is practically a mini-station in terms of capabilities. Normally, this is the point at which I would ask for volunteers, but it happens that Wylx, the second generation Stryx who inhabits the science ship in question, put in a special request right before I initiated this call."

"Wylx," Kelly mused out loud. "Why does that name sound so familiar?"

"Apparently it should, because Stryx Wylx requested that you be appointed the plenipotentiary tunnel network ambassador for the mission. I don't recall the exact wording of the message, but it was something about one good official request deserving another. I can't help wondering if it had to do with the high priority message about bedtimes that arrived from your embassy before this meeting."

"Oh, no! I just asked our station librarian to grant a pardon to one of her Stryx students who was misbehaving in my office, and Libby passed the request to his parent. Wylx must think I'm some kind of a busybody."

"Better you than me," Ambassador Zerakova said. "As exciting as a first contact with an unknown species sounds, a mission like that could turn into an open-ended commitment."

"It's lucky you have an associate ambassador to cover for you now," Belinda added. "I saw Daniel's promotion announced in the Galactic Free Press before it even showed up on the EarthCent organizational chart. How come Union Station is the only embassy with the associate position?"

"Daniel Cohan is a genuine pathfinder," the president said. "One day he'll promote himself to associate president and then I'll be able to take a long vacation."

"Wait a minute," Kelly objected. "Wylx requests my presence and I don't get any say in the matter?"

"You are eminently qualified," the Echo Station ambassador said soothingly. "I'll bet you've handled more first contacts than any other EarthCent ambassador since our introductory period on the tunnel network."

"I'm more interested in the high priority message about bedtimes," Ambassador Tamil declared with a yawn, and then cast a longing look at his empty coffee cup.

"I'm afraid it referred to children only, Raj," the president replied. "And while we're on the subject of parenting, I should point out that the Stryx have a special interest in this new species, which they apparently took under their wing some tens of thousands of years ago."

"Didn't you just say that the jump drive signature was unknown to the Stryx?" Ambassador Fu said.

"Yes, Zhao, but that's only because the technology is brand new, and Earth was the first known destination visited by the aliens. The Stryx informed me that the star system in question is actually one from a hidden reserve they keep for relocating promising species who are in danger of extinction from phenomena beyond their control. I won't pretend to understand the explanation, but it seems they employ some kind of multiverse origami to fold the space around the star system so that these new-comers could see out, but nobody could see in."

"How long ago did all of this happen?" Kelly asked the president.

"They didn't exactly load me down with details, but I'm sure Stryx Wylx will fill you in. In any case, the request made it clear that they expect you to put together a delega-tion, and I thought the other ambassadors might offer ideas on who you should bring."

"Wouldn't it be a good idea for her to take Hildy?" Am-bassador Enoksen suggested. "It couldn't hurt to have a public relations professional along."

"I'm afraid I can't do without Ms. Gruen for an indefi-nite period," the president replied shortly.

"How about representatives from some of our allies?" Belinda asked.

"That's up to Ambassador McAllister to negotiate with her colleagues. The mission will also be accompanied by one of the younger Stryx to give a physical presence to their views, as the newcomers may be uncomfortable negotiating with a disembodied voice."

"I would suggest you have your associate ambassador choose some representatives from his Sovereign Human Communities organization," Svetlana said. "They're used to working with aliens, and the ones I've met were fantastic salesmen."

"Do you think it would be classless to bring some of our spies along?" Ambassador White asked. "After all, we are the intelligence steering committee."

"As long as they identify themselves as intelligence agents," Zhao said. "It's likely the newcomers will have counterparts who will want to talk with them."

"It's a bit embarrassing that we don't have any military people to bring," Ambassador Tamil commented tiredly. "We must be the only species on the tunnel network without dress uniforms for formal occasions."

"Don't forget the journalists," the Middle Station ambassador reminded them. "You should really invite some Earth-based reporters in addition to the Galactic Free Press."

"Maybe a correspondent from the Children's News Network would make a good impression," Kelly ventured. "Could you suggest any candidates, Stephen? I know they come around your office all of the time."

"I'll ask for a couple who can spend that much time away from their families and put them on the next ship to Union Station," the president replied. "And you might want to bring some samples of Earth exports while you're at it. Maybe the new species won't be able to use anything, but it shows goodwill."

"I don't want to be a party pooper, but don't forget that they have developed their own faster-than-light technology," Ambassador Enoksen said. "They may not be as advanced as the species we're used to dealing with on the tunnel network, but they must be way ahead of us on most things."

"I hope for your sake they breathe an oxygen mix," Ambassador Zerakova pointed out. "I spent a few weeks in an encounter suit once and I wouldn't want to repeat the experience."

"The Stryx informed me that humans will be able to breathe the atmosphere without any filtering, and even better, the native foods can be eaten, though caution is advised," the president added.

"Seriously? Since when can we eat anybody else's food?" Kelly couldn't help asking.

"Don't look a gift horse in the mouth," Ambassador Fu advised her. "Enjoy your trip, and we look forward to hearing your report when you return."

Two

"...and so we'll be leaving as soon as Kevin lays in a stock of trade goods."

"Congratulations!" Flazint practically shouted, her face lighting up with joy for her friend. "It's awfully short notice for a wedding, but you can count on me to do anything you need to help. In Frunge families, the mother handles all of the preparations, but I know you guys aren't that traditional, and your mom is probably busy with her embassy and the new species and all."

"I don't think Dorothy mentioned marriage," Affie said cautiously. She took a sip from her fluorescent purple drink and braced herself for Flazint's reaction, which was quick to arrive.

"What?" the Frunge girl spluttered, her hair vines literally standing on end. "You're setting off on a trading voyage with a strange male and nobody but an underage dog for a chaperone?"

"Could I get another?" Dorothy asked the bartender. She had expected Flazint to be scandalized, but hearing it out loud still made her feel funny, especially after she had rejected as hopelessly bourgeoisie Kevin's suggestion that they get married before leaving. "He's been practically living in Mac's Bones for the last year and a half, so he's hardly a strange man. And Alexander is very mature for a two-year-old Cayl hound."

"It's not like they're just running off on a lark," Affie added. She paused for a moment to shake her head in polite rejection at a man sitting a few seats away who had been staring at her since the three fashion designers had come into the bar. "You know that Humans don't have as much time to waste on courting formalities as other species. Didn't you say that your mom and dad got married on their first date, Dorothy?"

"Exactly," the girl replied, taking a sip from her drink to fortify herself for her Frunge friend's inevitable objection.

"But they *did* get married," Flazint pointed out immediately. She was tempted to recite the long list of warnings about casual liaisons that had been drummed into her since childhood, but after correctly reading the nervousness in her friend's face, she relented. "Just let me see the contract," the Frunge girl said with a sigh. "At least I can make sure we won't have a repeat of the David incident."

Dorothy turned red and looked down at her drink, mumbling something about trust and mutual respect. Even Affie, who was the most bohemian of the three friends, was a little taken aback by the human's response. Before the Vergallian could put her objection into words, Flazint slammed her fist down on the bar, drawing looks from the patrons and staff alike.

"You are NOT going off in a spaceship with an unrelated man without at least a companionship contract!"

Dorothy had never seen her Frunge friend so angry and she felt her willpower failing, but she managed to mutter, "I'll do what I want."

"Look at me," Flazint demanded, taking Dorothy's face between her hands. "You're my friend, and I'm not going to let you destroy your life out of sheer obstinacy. I'll pay for the lawyer, all you have to do is sign it. Affie," she continued, turning to the Vergallian girl. "You go get Kevin and meet us at Hazint's legal shop. It's in the Frunge mercantile exchange corridor. Dorothy, you're coming with me."

"I just got this drink," the girl protested weakly, but Flazint now had an iron grip on Dorothy's wrist and dragged her out of the bar, much to the amusement of those who had been eavesdropping on the conversation. Affie polished off her purple concoction, paid the bartender, and headed for Mac's Bones to collect Kevin.

"I've never been so embarrassed," Dorothy grumbled after the pair entered the lift tube and her friend finally released her. She rubbed her wrist where Flazint's fingers had left white marks, and tried to think up a way out of the awkward situation that wouldn't offend the Frunge girl, but nothing came to mind.

"Don't be a baby," Flazint chided her. "The point of a companionship contract isn't to force you to do something you don't want to. If you can't come up with a few basic ground rules for conducting your relationship, it's clear you aren't ready to go running off together."

"Haven't you ever heard of spontaneity?"

"Not after a year and a half of shacking up," Flazint said, and it was the ambassador's daughter's turn to be shocked.

"You knew that we, uh…?

"I'm not an idiot, unlike some Human girls who I know. And one day I'm going to dance at your marriage party, whether you like it or not."

"Thanks, I guess," Dorothy said, touched by her friend's concern.

The capsule door slid open, and the two young women emerged on the Frunge commercial deck. Dorothy had to squint a little against the bright lighting as her pupils contracted to dots, and she felt the warmth of the amped-up infrared on her skin. Flazint led her past a number of expensive looking offices with frosted glass windows sporting alien calligraphy, and then stopped for a moment in front of an open set of scrollwork gates.

"Our honor court," the Frunge girl explained. "It's supposed to be built from hand-hewn stone, but that would just mean a façade on a space station, and what's the point of pretending? If either of you violates the terms of the contract, this is where the other party can come for justice."

"How can a Frunge court have jurisdiction over non-Frunge?" Dorothy asked. Humans living on the station generally assumed that the minimalistic rules laid out by the Stryx were the only law that counted, but she also knew that the various trading guilds and civic organizations were allowed to enforce their own rules on their own decks.

"What does the species have to do with jurisdiction?" Flazint replied. "If I went to your Earth and started committing crimes, would I get off free because I'm Frunge?"

"Of course not, but that's because you'd be in our jurisdiction."

"I suppose you could spend the rest of your life avoiding Frunge areas to get out of the contract, but we do have extradition treaties with most of the tunnel network species. We might even have one with Earth."

"Come on. What species would extradite somebody over violating a companionship contract? I mean, I'll sign it if it means that much to you, but I'm sure it's all stuff that Kevin and I already agree on."

"We'll see," Flazint said ominously. She guided Dorothy through another set of gates, nearly as impressive as those framing the courthouse doors. Behind the reception counter there was a work area where dozens of craftsmen were tending large industrial machines amidst a maze of tubing. The periphery of the office was lined with privacy booths, reminding Dorothy of a Vergallian fitting room. "This is Hazint's," the Frunge girl told Dorothy proudly.

"Are you here to register a domestic help contract?" the receptionist asked. "We have a boilerplate form for Human indentures that serves most situations without modification."

"I'm not a domestic," Dorothy protested. "We're here for a companionship contract."

The receptionist blanched and reached for the security button on her desk, but Flazint hastened to reassure her.

"There's another Human coming. They haven't developed companionship contracts yet and she's going off on a long trip with her boyfriend, so I thought…"

"I see," the receptionist interrupted, pulling her hand back from the alarm button, but not looking very pleased about the whole business. "You'll need to speak with Rzard, our expert in primitive cultures. Please have a seat in the waiting area and I'll notify him."

"She called me 'primitive,'" Dorothy complained. Flazint just shook her head, and the two young women settled down on a surprisingly comfortable bench constructed from some sort of springy metal mesh. "And I'm not going to wait all day for this, either."

"We just got here," Flazint soothed her. "Affie and Kevin haven't arrived yet, and I'm sure that if Rzard was otherwise engaged, the receptionist would have told us to make an appointment. Look, I'll bet that's him coming around the side of the work area now."

The front door of Hazint's swished open, and Affie entered with a puzzled-looking Kevin, who was wearing his standard jeans and a T-shirt.

"What's this all about, Dorothy?" he asked. "Your friend just said that I needed to come and sign something before you could leave the station."

"It seems that Flazint was upset by the idea of us traveling together without a, uh, more formal arrangement."

"Good for you," Kevin told the Frunge girl. "I've been trying to get her…"

"Welcome to Hazint's," a tired looking Frunge man interrupted. "I am Rzard, and I'll be your attorney of record. My billing on your case began the moment I left my office, so I recommend that you save the small talk for later. Shall we?"

Rzard turned abruptly and headed for the nearest privacy booth with an open door, the four young people trailing after him. As soon as they all entered, the attorney activated a privacy field, the door closed, and absolute silence prevailed. He then turned and looked expectantly at Flazint for an explanation. "Well?"

"My friend and co-worker, Dorothy McAllister, is leaving soon on a trading voyage with Kevin Crick." The Frunge girl didn't bother indicating the identified parties to the attorney as it would have insulted his intelligence.

"Why four names for just two people?" Rzard inquired.

"That's just the way they are," Affie interjected. "Some of them have three names, or even four."

"I see. So you wish to register a companionship contract?" he asked, again addressing himself to Flazint.

18

"Yes. I think the standard terms will be fine, except for the pollination and seedling clauses, of course."

"Of course." The attorney made some quick notes on a tab and then inquired without looking up, "Will you be establishing a schedule for intimate relations?"

"Huh?" Kevin grunted.

Dorothy cast an angry look at Flazint, who chose to studiously examine a seam between panels at the top of the privacy booth rather than meet her friend's eyes.

"Have I offended you?" Rzard asked. "My understanding is that Humans are continually fertile from an early age, and often engage in pre-marital relations."

"Not on a schedule," Dorothy managed to choke out.

"Will there be a number of offspring specified?" the attorney continued, unperturbed.

"We won't be gone that long," Kevin said, sounding confused. "It's just a shakedown cruise with a little vacation—maybe a month."

"I see," Rzard repeated. "So let's just run through the standard terms for a companionship, omitting the clauses specific to Frunge biology. By signing this agreement, you are committing to an exclusive relationship for the term of…"

Dorothy and Kevin exchanged looks, but Flazint spoke up, saying, "Six cycles."

"Indeed," Rzard responded, making a note and continuing. "For a period of, er, six cycles, Dorothy McAllister agrees to ensure that Kevin Crick is fed two meals per waking period…"

"Three," Kevin interrupted.

"Three meals per waking period, and provided with such support as required in his profession. She further—

19

no, that's not relevant here, er, no—six cycles, you say? It's hardly worth the effort."

Flazint glared at the attorney, who shrugged and continued. "Kevin Crick agrees to share equally with Dorothy McAllister any trading profits above overhead as defined in Frunge commercial code, provide a suitable budget for clothing and personal items, and—I don't believe that the terms involving ancestral offerings will apply either."

"Works for me," Kevin said. "Can I still do some of the cooking, though? I've got a lot more experience at it than Dorothy, especially in Zero-G."

"You cook?" the Frunge attorney asked in astonishment.

"It was either that or starve."

"I'm not sure which would be preferable," Rzard remarked, as if to himself. "Now, what assets are each of you bringing on this trip?"

"The ship and the trade goods are all Kevin's," Dorothy replied. "I'm bringing some samples from SBJ Fashions, but that's just in case we stumble into an opportunity."

"Actually, Shaina and Brinda are providing half of our cargo on consignment," Kevin told her. "I didn't have enough cash left to really stock up, and it doesn't make sense to fly around half empty."

"But I thought that part of trading was buying stuff," Dorothy objected. "Where will we put it all?"

"You have to sell to buy. Flying with empty space is the fastest way to go broke."

"Speaking of going broke, what gifts are you pledging to give the young lady?" the Frunge attorney inquired.

"You mean…something new?" Kevin asked.

"Do Humans have no culture of giving contract gifts?" Rzard cast an incredulous look at Flazint before ticking off on his fingers, "Jewelry, grow lights, precious metals, fine fabrics."

"Grow lights?" Kevin asked.

"Humans," Flazint reminded the attorney. "Their hair is dead as soon as it comes out."

"I see. No gifts then?"

All three girls turned to look at Kevin, who shifted uncomfortably in his chair. "I offered her an engagement ring, but she said it would interfere with the 3D modeling gloves she has to wear for work."

"So you take it off at work," Affie cried, staring at Dorothy in frustration.

"And will the young lady's family be supplying any provisions for the couple to begin housekeeping?" the attorney continued.

Now everybody shifted their attention to Dorothy, who said, "I could get a keg of beer from my dad, I guess."

"A keg of beer." Rzard shook his head mournfully. "I take it the two of you will be traveling alone."

"Alexander is coming with us," Kevin said. "He's used to sleeping on my bed."

The Frunge attorney gaped at the young man. "You wish to introduce a third party to this agreement? That won't do at all."

"Alexander is a Cayl hound," Flazint hastened to explain. "But he's not of age to be counted as a chaperone."

"One Cayl hound, underage," Rzard noted. "And who will be caring for said dog?"

"Oh, he takes care of himself, except for the opposable thumb stuff, like opening cans," Kevin replied.

"Of course," the attorney muttered. "Is the hound community property?"

21

"He adopted Kevin, but I do most of the petting," Dorothy said.

Rzard made some more notes on his pad, and then shrugged helplessly at Flazint. "Is there anything you want to add?"

"If by the expiration of this contract the parties fail to enter into marriage, Dorothy McAllister pledges to subscribe to the Eemas dating service and marry whoever the station librarian picks out for her."

"I'm not agreeing to that!" Dorothy exclaimed.

"We could just get married now," Kevin offered again.

"I want a real wedding reception, like the ball that Dring put on for my mom, but without all the diplomats."

"How much are you charging for time?" Affie asked Rzard, cutting short the argument.

The attorney pinched the side of his tab and held it up so that his clients could see the rapidly cycling numbers.

"Is that in Stryx creds?" Dorothy asked in a hushed tone.

The attorney nodded.

"Just print what you've got and we'll sign it," Kevin said.

Flazint broke into a wide grin and nodded at Rzard, who brought up a new screen with two blank boxes and handed Kevin a stylus.

"You sign in the top box. It's a Thark-bonded stylus and the agreement goes on record with them."

Kevin signed without hesitation, aware of the rapidly mounting cost.

"And you," Rzard said, accepting the stylus back from the young man and passing it to Dorothy. The girl's hand seemed to move of its own accord as she signed in the designated box. "And now the witnesses," the attorney continued, bringing up a new screen and pushing the tab and stylus to Flazint, who signed and passed them along to Affie.

"That's everything, then," Rzard declared. "Congratulations on your companionship, the contract will be waiting for you at the counter after you pay. And thank you for choosing Hazint's," he added in Flazint's direction. He quickly ushered them out of the booth and headed back towards his office.

"That wasn't so hard, was it?" Affie told her friend. She threw in a comforting rub between Dorothy's shoulder blades, as the girl seemed a little unsteady on her feet.

"What did I just agree to?" Dorothy asked.

"Happiness," Flazint said confidently, and then stepped in front of Kevin at the counter, producing a programmable cred. "I've got this."

"I can't let you pay for our, uh…" Kevin trailed off.

"Companionship contract," the Frunge girl said. "I'm the one who insisted Dorothy get one, and it's traditional to give a present to mark the occasion."

"But what if it doesn't work out?" Dorothy whispered to Affie.

"Don't worry," the Vergallian girl told her. "If I've learned one thing since I left home, it's that our paths in life aren't carved in stone."

Flazint approved the amount displayed by the Stryx register just as a workman appeared and placed a shallow plastic box on the counter. Kevin picked it up and grunted in surprise at the unexpected weight.

"Let's take a look," Flazint said happily, popping off the cover.

Dorothy stared at the Frunge characters cut deeply into the stone tablet and couldn't help wondering what kind of equipment worked so fast.

"High pressure water jets," Libby explained over the girl's implant. "Remember, six cycles, and then you have to marry whoever I pick out."

"You should join EarthCent Intelligence if you want to spy on people," Dorothy subvoced back. "Anyway, I'm marrying Kevin—eventually. I just didn't want it to look like we were doing it all of a sudden, like I was in trouble or something."

"There's many a slip twixt the cup and the lip," the Stryx librarian pronounced.

Three

"Rabbit food again?" the slender girl asked her lunch companion.

"I'm trying every option on the Vergallian vegan menu for a research project," Samuel replied. He chose a pre-pared salad from the case and slid it onto his tray before following Vivian down the counter.

"You must be the only student in the history of the Open University with a double major in Space Engineering and Vergallian Studies," Vivian said, pushing her own tray along until they reached the serious entrees. "Let's see," the girl continued, studying the steam-table pans in the human-safe section. "I'll have the goulash, and plenty of bread."

"Can I get some bread too?" Samuel asked the four-armed server.

"Bread is only free with full entrees," the towering Dollnick female replied as she glowered down at the young man's tray. "It will cost you fifty centees."

"Just eat some of mine," the girl said in exasperation. "Why do you think I took so much?"

The Dollnick gave Vivian a scowl and stretched out one of her upper arms to snatch back a roll, but the girl skipped out of reach to the dessert section.

"Looks like fruit salad for us again," Samuel groaned, after surveying the large array of choices, the majority of which were fatal to humans. "Am I missing anything?"

"You wouldn't have any chocolate chip cookies hidden back there, would you?" Vivian asked the Gem counter-woman, though she seemed to be pointing up at the ceiling with her index finger, rather than indicating the display case.

"I don't see any," the clone replied innocently, flashing Vivian a peace sign.

"I'm sure you could find a couple if you looked," Vivian cajoled, displaying her own peace sign while pretending to rub her ear, but with one finger bent forward at the knuckle.

The Gem nodded, reached under the counter with a pair of tongs, and drew out two enormous chocolate chip cookies. She deposited them on a pre-cut square of plastic film, wrapped them together, and handed them over the counter to the girl.

"Thank you," Vivian said, dropping a cred and a fifty-centee piece in the tip jar before moving forward to the drinks section. She slid the wrapped cookies into her purse.

"I wish you wouldn't do that," Samuel grumbled. "My mom says that bribing counter workers for off-menu perks at places with a cash register just encourages corruption."

"The rest of the species have a very different definition for corruption than your mother. I'm surprised you haven't covered that by now in your Vergallian Studies course. And I can eat both cookies if it will save you from a guilty conscience."

"I didn't say that," the boy protested, glancing down at his salad. Humans could survive on a Vergallian vegan

26

diet, but most wouldn't call it living. "Still not drinking coffee?"

"I promised my mom to wait until I'm sixteen," Vivian replied. "I think she's worried that I'll turn into a total addict, like my dad."

Samuel guiltily filled a mug with steaming black coffee, a drink that was almost as popular with several of the alien species as it was with humans, and placed it on his tray. Vivian took a bottle of Union Station Springs mineral water from a pan filled with crushed ice.

"I know you have money and everything, but why do you pay for that stuff?" the ambassador's son scoffed. "It's the same water you can get for free out of the cafeteria fountain, and they don't charge for the cups."

"It is not the same water," the girl insisted. She turned the bottle in her hand and began reading the label out loud. "Triple-filtered through the finest sand and oxygenated by a natural waterfall, Union Station Springs mineral water is a cut above." She placed the bottle on her tray triumphantly.

"A cut above what?" Samuel objected. "And you know exactly what waterfall they're talking about. It's the one on the wastewater treatment…"

"Lah, lah, lah, lah, lah," Vivian sang, placing her hands over her ears.

"Come on. You're holding up the line," a Drazen complained loudly. "It's bad enough that I'm stuck behind a Verlock without the two of you making a big production over choosing your lunch. Besides, this cafeteria is for students, and little Miss Songbird doesn't look old enough to be in here."

"Easy, Gorb," the Drazen's companion said to him. "That girl is kicking my butt in Dynastic Studies. She's one of those pierogies."

"Prodigies," the Verlock student corrected the Drazen as the young humans moved ahead to the register.

"I'll get this," Samuel said. "I got a big tip at the lost-and-found last night for returning an egg to a Huktra. We reran the security imaging and it turned out that one of the early hatchlings pushed it out of the nest when the mother was taking a brooding break. A maintenance bot assumed the egg was lost and brought it in."

"I didn't know we had any of those dragons living on the station."

"I think she's sort of a refugee," the boy replied, handing a ten-cred coin to the Horten cashier and indicating both trays. "She's staying on the park deck that the Gem abandoned before their old empire fell. Libby said that Gryph made the Huktra promise not to eat any sentients."

"Then you better not go near her," the eavesdropping Drazen cracked, and then dissolved in laughter at his own joke.

Samuel ignored the jibe, accepted his change, and surveyed the grid of cafeteria tables for two empty places. Vivian undertook a blocking maneuver to prevent Samuel from approaching a table occupied by Vergallian students and steered him instead to side-by-side vacancies with a mixed group consisting of Frunge, Grenouthians, and a Verlock. The alien students were engaged in an energetic argument when the humans arrived.

"Competency tests are the only thing that matters," a beefy bunny stated with finality. The two other Grenouthians at the table were too well brought up to voice their support with their mouths full, but they glared at the Frunge students, who apparently disagreed with the first bunny's position.

"Just because the Open University has always done it that way doesn't mean that there aren't alternatives," an attractive Frunge female protested. "In our metallurgy schools at home, students can take a certificate for successfully smelting different ores…"

"So it's still a test," the same Grenouthian interrupted.

"But it's not an all-at-once thing," the girl continued. "Some students get through the basics in a few cycles, others need several times that. As long as they master the basic techniques…"

"You'll end up with more dross than pure metal that way," the bunny interrupted again. "Can't you understand that aptitude is more than just a head start? It's amazing your species ever got into space with that wishy-washy attitude."

"Humans give partial credit," the Verlock rumbled loudly. The other students paused to give him a chance to continue, but he had spoken just before raising another slab of a leathery substance to his mouth, and was already engaged in chewing.

"You two look like Humans," the Frunge girl said, turning to Samuel and Vivian. "What's partial credit?"

"We went to school on the station," Samuel replied. "I think it's an Earth thing, like grading on a curve."

"Earth tests all include trigonometry?" the Grenouthian asked skeptically. "I have a hard time believing that. Your species is notoriously bad at math."

"No, my dad said they used a grading curve for everything when he was in school," Samuel explained. "Like, if you had a test where a perfect score was a hundred but the best student got eighty, then eighty became a perfect score."

One of the Frunge students was so stunned that he forgot to swallow properly and began to choke. The burly bunny next to him thumped the Frunge on the back, causing a piece of meat to dislodge from his throat and shoot across the table, where it bounced off of Vivian's shoulder. The girl deftly caught it with her spoon before it could fall into her goulash, and reached across the table to deposit it back on the Frunge's plate. Then she carefully wiped off the spoon on her napkin before continuing to eat.

"You're joking about grading on a curve, right?" the Frunge girl demanded.

Samuel swallowed a mouthful of salad, as much to save himself from having to prolong the tasteless mastication experience as to clear his mouth, and replied, "No. And the way my dad described it, they didn't want to make any of the students feel bad about themselves, so they did the same thing with the bottom of the curve."

"They gave the students with no correct answers perfect scores?" the bunny demanded, his eyes bugging out. "That explains a lot."

"No, no," Samuel protested, employing his Vergallian chopsticks to play with his salad while hungrily eyeing Vivian's goulash. "They made the bottom of the curve the average, so everybody scored between average and outstanding. My mom said it was the same at the university she went to before the Stryx recruited her."

Vivian sighed and broke a roll in half. Then she carefully spooned some meat out of her goulash and passed the improvised sandwich to Samuel, who accepted it with a guilty look of thanks.

"Let me get this straight," the Frunge girl said. "They had tests, but everybody passed? What's the point of that?"

Samuel took his time chewing his first bite of the savory stew sandwich before responding. "Not everybody. They took attendance or something, and if you didn't come to class enough, you got an incomplete and you had to take the course again."

"Different now," the Verlock said. Like most students of his species at the Open University, he had learned to minimize the number of words in his utterances to participate in mixed-species conversations. "Academies and teacher bots. My seventh cousin works on Earth."

"Humans let other species run schools on your homeworld?" one of the other bunnies asked.

"I met a kid there who grew up where there weren't any schools nearby, so he just studied with a teacher bot," Samuel replied. "He recently became a journalist for the Galactic Free Press, and I saw him on the station if you want to talk to him about it. I know that EarthCent invited the Verlocks to set up an alternative education network on Earth, and Astria's Academy of Dance…"

"Every planet on the tunnel network has some of those," the Frunge girl interrupted. "I can understand bots for students whose families can't afford real teachers, but bringing in aliens to run your schools just seems weird."

"Like hiring aliens to babysit for your children?" Vivian countered.

"Hey, have you seen InstaSitter's latest commercial?" the third Grenouthian asked. Everybody turned to the bunny like he was offering an inside tip on the upcoming Horten gaming championships. The student made the most of his time in the spotlight by acting out the whole ad, concluding with, "…and then, when the couples from

31

all of those different species are taking their seats at the opera, a voiceover says, 'Without InstaSitter, life itself would be impossible.'"

Out of the corner of his eye, Samuel noticed Vivian mouthing the words as the bunny spoke them.

"Good business, InstaSitter," the Verlock remarked, then added sadly, "No public shares."

A Dollnick student chose that moment to approach their table. "Hey, can you guys spare a moment?"

"Are you selling wax-coated Sheezle larvae or something equally disgusting?" the Frunge girl asked suspiciously.

"I'm an activist," the alien said proudly. "We're petitioning the Stryx to include student representatives from all of the tunnel network members on the mission to the latest species that tested a faster-than-light drive. I heard that they have four arms."

"Waste of time," the Verlock declared, and lifted another slab of food from his plate. "Stryx won't change."

"Well, we have to try, don't we?" the Dollnick said with undiminished enthusiasm. "In addition to a petition, we're planning a rally with music and dancing on the next partial convergence day. It just doesn't make any sense to leave something as important as choosing members for a tunnel network invitation mission to the Humans."

The Frunge girl grabbed one of the excited Dollnick's hands to get his attention and indicated Samuel and Vivian with a tilt of her head, but the large alien kept right on with his pitch.

"It's not just the commercial opportunities, though those are obviously important. It's about making a good first impression. Just imagine if you'd never seen an alien before and the Stryx sent a Human delegation to your world. You'd probably start shooting as soon as they came out of the ship!" Some untranslatable whistles of laughter escaped the Dollnick at his own joke, and a couple of the Grenouthians couldn't help grinning, but the Frunge girl stood on her chair and whispered something in the activist's ear.

"Oh, sorry," the Dollnick addressed Vivian and Samuel. "I thought you were Vergallians. You should really come up with a system to keep the rest of us from getting confused, like wearing different color hats or something."

"My mom is the EarthCent ambassador, and she didn't say anything about the newcomers having four arms," Samuel said calmly. "And she didn't ask for the mission either. We're stuck with it because the alien ship jumped into our homeworld's system."

"I heard that the new species lives in hydroponic tanks," one of the other Frunge students offered. "Supposedly they evolved from seaweed or something."

"That would make an interesting documentary," the biggest Grenouthian remarked. "Hey, do you think your mom would go for an upgraded visual implant if we paid for it? My dad works for the network, and I'll bet they'd be happy to do it in exchange for exclusive footage."

"So what about my petition?" the Dollnick pressed on. "You guys can sign it too if you want," he added, offering a bonded tab to Vivian. "No hard feelings."

"No hard feelings," Vivian repeated, ignoring the tab.

All three of the Grenouthians signed, followed by the Frunge students. One of them felt she had to offer Samuel an explanation, and said, "It's not that we have anything against your mom or Humans. It's just that we're for us, too."

"I understand," Samuel said. "When is that rally coming up?"

"End of the current cycle," the Dollnick replied. "Tickets are five creds now, ten creds at the door," he added hopefully.

"I'm pretty sure that my mom is leaving before then," Samuel informed him. "And I agree with our Verlock friend that the Stryx aren't going to change their decision because a bunch of Open University students throw a big party."

"What kind of music?" Vivian asked.

"Uh, you know, dancing music. It's not really my thing," the alien admitted, looking from one human to the other. "Are you sure about the timing of the mission?"

"I'll take two," Vivian said, fishing a ten-cred coin from her change purse. "Vivian Oxford and Samuel McAllister," she declared for the Dollnick's tab to record the cash purchase.

"You don't really expect me to dance at a rally against my own mother's mission," Samuel protested.

"I want to pay you back for lunch. Besides, she'll be gone by then, so it's kind of moot."

"We might try to move it up," the Dollnick said.

"That's silly," Vivian told him. "If you don't hold it on a convergence day, who's going to come? A bunch of Dollnicks? You guys run the weirdest daylight hours of any species on the station."

"She's right," the biggest Grenouthian affirmed. "Dollnicks are always out of synch when we do live shows."

"Yeah, let me have a pair of tickets too," the Frunge girl said. Instead of handing over a coin, she pulled out her university tab and tapped a couple of symbols, transferring the money to the Dollnick's tab.

The Grenouthian students had all finished eating by this point and rose with their trays as the activist moved on to the next group. A couple of humans took their places at the end of the table. The friendly Frunge turned her head from one side to the other, remarking, "I feel like a Bliznick," causing the hair vines of her two companions to rustle in silent laughter.

"What's a Bliznick?" Vivian asked.

"A type of cookie made from two pieces of cured meat sandwiching fermented cheese," the Frunge explained. "I'm the cheese in this scenario."

"Thanks for reminding me." Vivian opened her purse and retrieved the chocolate chip cookies. She undid the plastic wrap and passed one to Samuel.

"Those look yummy," one of the newly arrived students said. She lifted up her bowl of fruit salad and offered, "Any chance you'd take this for half a cookie?"

"The Gem might have some left," Vivian told the student. "They're all chocoholics, and since it's a relatively new thing for them, they get most of their recipes from us. She usually brings in some homemade desserts that humans can eat to supplement her income."

"It's kind of under the counter," Samuel added.

"So you pay through the tip jar, like at the canteen," the girl surmised, nodding her understanding. "What's the going rate?"

Vivian again flashed the bent knuckle peace sign, adding, "For two." She broke her cookie in half, rewrapped one part in plastic, and slid it down the table to the newcomer. "No, keep the fruit salad. Just tell me what we can get from the canteen. I went in once and I didn't see anything."

"The Drazen employees order take-out pizzas from the good place in the Little Apple and resell it by the slice as a side business. But they get hot peppers on everything, so be careful."

"Do we just say we want pizza?" Samuel asked, forgetting his objection to unauthorized selling.

"Earth wedges," the girl answered. "And if you order two slices, make sure you say, 'Two Earth wedges, colors up,' or they'll slap 'em together like a sandwich and you won't be able to pick off the hot peppers."

Four

"What are you doing here, Jeeves?" Kelly asked. She wasn't really that surprised to see the Stryx in the meeting room as she knew that Libby was attempting to groom her offspring for diplomacy, and the station librarian was used to getting her way.

"I got drafted to serve as Wylx's boots on the ground. Some species get spooked by voices that seem to originate out of nowhere, and according to extensive research and testing, my current form is very nonthreatening, especially when I use the treads rather than floating."

"Is that why you keep them? I always wondered if they were like a vestigial growth."

"Where do you think robot bodies come from?" Jeeves asked, sounding genuinely curious.

"I haven't thought about it, really. I've never seen you break down, so your body must be really well made."

Despite his lack of lungs, Jeeves generated the audio equivalent of a deep sigh. "We manufacture them ourselves, of course. The basic barrel-and-treads design was a built-in configuration supplied by the Makers, so young Stryx usually stick with it for a few thousand years to show respect for our roots. But it's all about field manipulation in the end. This body just provides a focal point and a place to put things."

"I knew it was something like that," Kelly said, not really listening beyond the first sentence of the explanation. "So you'll be coming on my mission?"

"I think you meant to thank us for inviting you on our mission."

"Do either of you need a secretary?" asked the Drazen ambassador as he entered the room. "Or taster? I'm very good at screening out harmful poisons in new environments."

"Ambassador McAllister is in charge of the biological contingent," Jeeves replied. "I'm sure she'll establish a formal application process in keeping with protocol."

"It seems to me that any species which can survive exposure to Humans would be happy to welcome me," the Vergallian ambassador said, arriving right behind Bork. "If need be, I could get some prosthetics and try to pass as Human. A bad dental insert, a wig, and perhaps some heavy make-up might do the trick."

"But your eyes, my dear, are too beautiful to be disguised," declared the alien following on her heels.

"Ortha!" Kelly greeted the Horten ambassador, who had always had an affinity for the Vergallian beauties. "I thought you..." she trailed off.

"You thought I was fired and in disgrace," the silver-tongued diplomat completed the EarthCent ambassador's sentence. "I was placed on suspension for ten cycles after committing my people to paying back the Stryx for our piracy liability exposure. But in the end, it was decided that my experience was too valuable to throw on the scrap heap."

"It sounds to me like your pension had already vested," Bork insinuated.

"Somebody at the home office may have done the math and concluded that with my time in service, it's cheaper to keep me working," the Horten ambassador admitted. "Since a diplomat of my seniority has veto power over new assignments, we reached a compromise that brings me to Union Station for another tour."

"I'm just glad you're back, Ortha," Kelly said unashamedly.

"Did somebody say that Ortha's back?" the Frunge ambassador asked as he entered the room. "I don't know what's wrong with our intelligence service lately. It's bad enough they couldn't tell me anything about this new species. How hard can it be to keep track of Horten diplomatic postings?"

"Ortha's return was on our morning broadcast," a large bunny remarked, elbowing his way past Czeros and heading for the large chair labeled, "Grenouthian Ambassador."

"But when did your morning start?" the Frunge retorted.

"A couple of beats ago," the ambassador replied, not specifying whether he meant Stryx beats, heartbeats, or something else. "The point is, we were the first to report it."

"I wouldn't fault your people for not knowing anything about a previously unheard-of species," Abeva said to Czeros. "All that our own intelligence service could come up with is a profile suggesting that the newcomers suffer from poor taste."

"Based on what?" Kelly demanded.

"Their choice of a destination for testing a jump drive," the Vergallian replied sweetly, leading Ortha and the arriving Dollnick ambassador to chuckle.

"Catering," a clone announced from the doorway. All of the diplomats looked over eagerly, but it was just the Gem ambassador playing on their prejudices.

"You've got to stop doing that," the Grenouthian ambassador complained. "False alarms wreak havoc with my digestive system."

"Sorry I'm only just on time," Srythlan announced, edging his way through the door. "I hope you started without me."

"We're just waiting on the Fillinduck," Jeeves said, tallying up the ambassadors with his pincer.

"He never comes to meetings that I attend, and the Chert isn't here yet either," Kelly pointed out, slapping the seat of the empty chair next to hers. "Oh. Sorry."

The Chert ambassador materialized and bent over to pick up the gaming device that Kelly had knocked out of his hands. He gave the EarthCent ambassador a scowl.

"I'm sure you're all aware by now that another species in this neck of the galaxy has broken the faster-than-light barrier, thus becoming eligible for an invitation to join the tunnel network," Jeeves began. "The mission will be undertaken by Stryx Wylx, and I'll be accompanying to serve as her mouthpiece. Ambassador McAllister has been chosen to head the biological delegation as the first jump destination chosen by the newcomers was the Sol system. Any questions?"

"I'm sure we've all been consulting our historical records, and when the Stryx sent a mission to invite us to join the tunnel network, it was just the Frunge," Bork said.

"What do you mean by 'Just the Frunge'?" Czeros demanded.

"Sorry, Ambassador. I meant we were visited by a Frunge delegation that arrived in a Frunge ship. No science ship, no posse of aliens, no young Stryx prank-sters."

"Same here," Ortha remarked. "I hope the Frunge were getting a commission."

"My own people were contacted by a Verlock," Abeva chipped in. "Even with perfect translation devices on both sides, the talks repeatedly broke down due to long silenc-es."

"It is the Verlock way to allow time for thought during negotiations," Srythlan said.

"According to my report, the queen leading our negoti-ating team conceived and gave birth during one of your pauses," the Vergallian ambassador retorted.

"We were initially approached by the Grenouthians," Clume said, casting an angry look down the table. "The only surviving record of the encounter is their documen-tary, 'Four arms, zero brains.'"

"You have to remember that the subject of a documen-tary is never the primary audience," the Grenouthian ambassador told the Dollnick, and then turned to Jeeves. "I think the point we're all trying to make, young Stryx, is that sending a science ship on a welcoming mission is not standard procedure."

"Your invitations all went out before my time," Jeeves replied. "There are some special considerations involved in this case. The species in question had already been inter-fered with—I'm sorry—aided by the Stryx during their formative years."

"That area of space had already been independently surveyed by our ships and marked as empty, so we know you're talking about a hidden reserve," Clume said, and several of the other ambassadors confirmed this assess-ment.

41

"Yes, it's one of Gryph's systems as it happens," Jeeves replied. "I'm not at liberty to share all of the data, but Wylx transferred this species to their current home at a time that their recordkeeping was limited to campfire stories and cave drawings. She also transported sufficient populations of the flora and fauna of their birthplace to ensure a viable ecosystem. The Alts, as we call them, were left alone as soon as it became clear that they had adjusted to their new world. Other than passive monitoring, we have had no contact with them since."

"Why did they choose Earth for their first jump?" Kelly asked.

"Proximity," Srythlan answered, amazing the others by being the first to respond. "They're practically next door to you."

"I thought the system was hidden," Kelly objected.

"An update showing the location has been pushed out to all Stryx-built ship controllers," Crute explained.

"Then what's to keep you all from going there on your own?"

"The update clearly labels the system as 'off limits pending membership tender,' an underhanded maneuver if you ask me," the Grenouthian ambassador grumbled. "Our news network paid a pile of creds to a Dollnick freighter captain for the recorded jump telemetry, and our scientists had already narrowed down the likely point of origin to within ten light years."

"Assuming the Alts join the tunnel network, you'll all have the chance to visit them soon enough," Jeeves continued. "I invited everybody to this meeting to make sure you were aware of the current travel ban, and to inform you that I am authorized to carry one message from each of you to the new species."

"How many words?" the Chert ambassador asked.

"Will a one-shot holocube be acceptable?" Ortha inquired eagerly.

"Are you planning to relay their responses, or are you just offering for the sake of seeing what we come up with?" the Gem ambassador asked.

"Good question," several of the other ambassadors complimented the clone.

"If the Alts wish to send a response, I solemnly swear to see that you get it," Jeeves said. "But to be perfectly honest, I suspect your time would be better spent persuading Ambassador McAllister to invite you along."

"What did I do to deserve this?" Kelly asked in dismay, as all of the diplomats at the table pivoted in her direction. The Chert quickly removed his shoulder-mounted invisibility projector and nudged it in front of her on the table, like a gift offering. "EarthCent has a policy against ambassadors accepting bribes," she told him.

"But when you turn it on, nobody will be able to see it," the Chert ambassador said, puzzled by her objection.

"I have far too much respect for your integrity to offer a bribe," Czeros said to Kelly. "Unless you want one, that is."

"What the Frunge ambassador means is that he doesn't have a fixed budget for diplomatic purchases," Abeva interjected. "I, on the other hand, am backed by the wealth of the Empire of a Hundred Worlds."

"Stop!" Kelly demanded, half-rising from her seat. "I don't know what the Stryx are up to here, but I'm sure that me cherry-picking representatives from every oxygen-breathing species on the tunnel network isn't going to make anybody happy. Besides, when the Stryx opened Earth, they just showed up, took over our communications networks, and talked directly to the people. How come the Alts are getting special treatment?"

"Aren't you forgetting something, Ambassador?" Bork asked gently.

Kelly sat back down and studied the Drazen's face for clues while the other ambassadors displayed unusual patience. "You mean the whole protectorate thing? The fact we never developed our own jump drive and needed to be rescued from ourselves? No, and I also haven't forgotten that all of you treated me like a leper when I first came to Union Station, and that was like fifty years after the Stryx opened Earth."

"Humans are an acquired taste," Bork admitted. "Besides, we weren't exactly welcome on Earth until just a few years ago. How many extraterrestrials did you see growing up?"

"None," Kelly admitted. "But what makes you all so interested in the Alts, anyway? Maybe they're poor farmers with one brilliant scientist who created a jump drive."

"It doesn't work that way," Ortha said. "Faster-than-light-travel is a product of high economic and technological achievement, and the home system of a species which has just made the breakthrough is usually densely populated, which creates all sorts of business opportunities."

"Independently conceived mathematical models of the universe are of great interest to scholars," Srythlan added.

"Not to mention the potential for important new documentaries," the Grenouthian ambassador said. Kelly's translation implant made the giant bunny sound so earnest that the plea caught her off guard. Then she remembered that the Grenouthian network had no objection to paying a finder's fee in the way of production points to career diplomats.

"The steady improvement of humanity's economic fortunes is making it more expensive for us to find contract laborers," Crute pointed out, and Bork nodded in agreement. "The Alts will likely want to earn Stryx creds to purchase things from tunnel network species, and may even be interested in trading labor for an equity position in one or more of our terraforming projects."

"So you're saying you all want to come along, and you're not worried about the mission stretching out for months?" Kelly asked.

"What's to stretch?" Abeva said dismissively. "Either they'll be overjoyed by the invitation or they'll attack us."

"As our four-armed friends did when we first visited them," the Grenouthian ambassador added.

"The Alts are remarkably peaceful for biologicals," Jeeves told the others. "They have no history of internecine strife, and we have observed no signs of weapons in their shipbuilding program."

"So they may be in the market for some," the Dollnick ambassador said.

"They never fought amongst themselves?" Srythlan asked slowly. "Are they a race of empaths?"

"That would be a difficult thing to determine from a distance through instrumentality," the Stryx replied evasively. "I would suggest that those members of the delegation who wear dress weapons to formal occasions consider leaving the hardware at home."

"How many delegation members can I choose, Jeeves?" Kelly asked in a tired voice.

"As many as you please, Ambassador. Wylx can reconfigure her interior at will to make space for any number of guests. But I would remind you that when it comes to making a good impression, there is always a point of diminishing returns."

"What do you mean?"

"Just think about your relations with your colleagues in the room," Jeeves suggested. "A bar of chocolate might improve your standing with the Gem ambassador, but a shipload would just make her nervous."

"For a shipload of chocolate, I'll be your pet," the clone offered.

"Maybe that wasn't the ideal example," Jeeves admitted. "Let's say you wanted to score points with the Frunge ambassador by offering him a bottle of..."

"You're really not very good with hypothetical examples, are you?" Kelly interrupted, as Czeros stared daggers at the young Stryx.

"Your children would have understood me the first time," Jeeves grumbled. "I'm trying to convey that there's a difference between a peaceful delegation and an invasion."

"So why didn't you say that in the first place?"

"Because I'm practicing being DIPLOMATIC!" Jeeves thundered.

"Good job," Abeva observed dryly. "Now perhaps we can return to the important business of filling out the mission personnel? As the ambassador of the most populous of the humanoid species on the tunnel network, I am pleased to offer my services in any executive capacity required."

"I just want a straight answer from Jeeves first on how many of you I can invite along before I make any choices," Kelly replied.

"The group of ambassadors present would make an impressive display without being overwhelming," the Stryx acknowledged after a pause.

"That settles it," the Grenouthian ambassador declared, hopping up and moving towards the exit. "Lots to prepare before we leave. Thank you for the invitation, Ambassador McAllister."

"You've chosen well," Abeva said, pushing back her chair. "I'll see you all on Wylx's ship."

"Likewise," the Chert mumbled, snatching back his invisibility projector and disappearing.

"Why isn't there ever any catering when I come to one of these meetings?" the Gem ambassador asked plaintively, rising from her seat. "Pending consultation with my sisters, I tentatively accept your request, Ambassador McAllister."

"I couldn't have timed my return any better," Ortha said, looking rather smug. He flashed Kelly a thumbs-up and followed the others out.

"The princes will want to know about my appointment immediately," the Dollnick ambassador announced, taking his leave.

Kelly shook her head as if trying to clear it, and then looked around the conference table at the remaining ambassadors. "Did any of you hear me invite any of them?"

"Too late now," Bork told her cheerfully. "You can invite me twice if it makes you feel any better."

"I don't know if I'm doing you a favor or an injury, but you are all invited. At least Jeeves will have somebody else to pester."

"Serious undertaking, invitation mission," Srythlan remarked. "Most species reject the first offer."

"Really? Why would they do that?" Kelly inquired.

"Pride, I expect," Czeros responded. "Imagine you had just conquered the challenge of interstellar flight and a

47

delegation of aliens suddenly showed up at your world. I wouldn't be surprised if the reason the Alts left your system so quickly is that they detected the tunnel network entrance and realized they were hopelessly outclassed."

"But as soon as we show up, they'll know that we know where they live," the EarthCent ambassador pointed out. "I don't want to sound like I'm presenting them with an ultimatum when I haven't even met them, but what choice do they have?"

"When we send a mission to invite a species to join the tunnel network, it comes with the option to indefinitely postpone accepting and to be left alone by the other tunnel network species in the interim," Jeeves replied. "While we aren't technically committed to preventing non-members from visiting their system, I suspect that in this case, Gryph would simply hide them again."

Five

"This is silly," Dorothy fumed. "I've been off the station in small spaceships plenty of times. Let's just go already."

"Approaching the tunnel entrance," Kevin repeated in a stern voice. "Fasten your safety harness."

"I am not strapping myself in with a four-point restraint and pretending we're in space," the girl retorted. "Look. Beowulf climbed on top of the wrecker so he can see in through the port, and he's laughing at us."

Alexander added a sharp bark from the dog bed, where Kevin had secured him with light cargo netting.

"Sorry," Dorothy said, glancing over her shoulder at the dog. "I guess Beowulf is laughing at Alex, but the point is that we all look like idiots."

Kevin sighed and turned to Dorothy. "We agreed to a twenty-four-hour dry run to make sure you were up to this. Now that we're underway, I'm the captain, and if you continue to disobey my direct orders, I'll have to throw you in the brig."

"We are NOT underway and you do NOT have a brig. What are you going to do? Throw a net over me like the poor dog?"

"It's to keep him from floating around while he's sleeping in Zero-G," the young man explained, and then changed tack. "Proper preparation means a lot to me. If you absolutely can't do it, then we'll leave now, but imagine how you'd feel if you couldn't test-fit clothes on your models before a fashion show."

"They're all the same size anyway—skinny," Dorothy replied darkly. "Wait. Am I a fashion model in your analogy?"

"Uh, yes?" Kevin ventured.

"Oh, all right," she said, buckling her safety harness. "We can play spaceman if it will make you feel better, but twelve hours and then we're leaving."

"Great. Now let me show you how the manual backup systems work in case the controller is disabled. Ship. Run tunnel transit simulation."

While Kevin drilled Dorothy in the functions of the various gesture controls for the holo interface, Alexander crept out from under the edge of the webbing on his basket and sat behind them, mimicking their motions with his fore-paws. Outside the ship, Beowulf was joined on top of the wrecker by Joe and Paul, all three of them enjoying the free show immensely.

By the end of two hours, Kevin was saying "Excellent," far more often than, "You almost got it," and Dorothy was beginning to feel like she could fly the ship without either him or the controller. After a final flawless run through the simulation, she undid the four-point restraint and got up to stretch.

"Ready for a turn on the exercise machines?" Kevin asked.

"I've got to use the bathroom," she replied, heading for the main hatch.

"You just walked past the access door. It's the green button that glows red when somebody is in there."

"I am NOT going to use the Zero-G sanitary equipment when there's a perfectly good bathroom with plumbing just a two-minute walk from here. I mean, even you have to be reasonable."

"I give up. Go home to use the bathroom and then we're leaving."

"Do you want anything else from the house?" Dorothy called over her shoulder after popping the hatch.

"I guess a sandwich would be good," Kevin allowed. "And some fruit? Never mind. I'll just come along and give Alexander a chance to run off some energy before we leave."

Five hours later, Kevin had to bribe Beowulf to sniff out Alexander. The young Cayl hound had figured out that his people were serious about leaving the comforts of Union Station and hid in Dring's garden to give them an opportunity to reconsider. By the time the ship entered the tunnel bound for Drazen space, it was nearly midnight, local human time.

"I shouldn't have eaten all of those desserts Aisha made," Dorothy groaned.

"If you have to sick up, use the bag."

"Tell me again why we're here?"

"I'm a trader, Dorothy, and as much as I liked working with your Dad and Paul, I don't want to be their third wheel for the rest of my life. Aren't you excited about visiting the worlds of some of your friends from Union Station?"

"I'll be dead before we ever get out of the tunnel. This is awful."

"Try breathing into the sick bag," Kevin advised her. "You're starting to hyperventilate." He watched in concern for a few minutes as the bag crinkled in and out, and eventually her respiration slowed. "I got some patches from the Farling that he said would help with space sickness if you're desperate, but I wanted to give you a chance to acclimate naturally."

"What?" Dorothy demanded, ripping the bag away from her face. "You have a Zero-G cure and you didn't tell me about it?"

"I don't know if it will work, and it's just putting off the inevitable. In a few days your body will…"

"I want it NOW!"

"All right. All right. I've got the first-aid kit here somewhere." Kevin pushed off his seat and floated over to one of the bridge lockers, where he quickly located the white metal box and withdrew a waxy sheet covered with circular patches. "Doc said that it's a time-release patch that allows the medicine to be absorbed through your skin, so it may take a while to reach its full potency."

"Everything is spinning too much, you put it on me," the girl begged.

Kevin peeled one of the patches from the sheet and carefully stuck it on the side of Dorothy's neck. "He warned me that there may be a stimulative side effect, like drinking several cups of coffee. The drug he derived it from is actually banned on Stryx stations because it's addictive, but the doc is pretty sure he eliminated that part."

"Pretty sure?" Dorothy asked, already sounding a little better. She peered at him blearily, but managed to keep both of her eyes open together for the first time since they'd entered the tunnel.

"Well, you're sort of the first person to try it," Kevin admitted. "I didn't even know there were such things as Zero-G cures. The Farling said that space sickness isn't uncommon in poorly designed humanoids, and that it can take a few hundred generations to breed it out."

"I feel better already," Dorothy declared, and even gambled on a peek out the viewport. "It's just black. Where are the stars?"

"I don't know, it's always dark in the tunnels. You're the one with the Stryx education."

"I didn't like any of that fancy math stuff and Libby didn't force it on us. It takes most humans a lifetime just to learn the basics, and by that time, we're too old to do anything with it. Hey, I think I'm getting hungry."

"I don't think eating is such a great idea when you were ready to hurl just a few minutes ago. It's already after midnight and nothing ever happens in the tunnels, so why don't we try to get some sleep?"

"You go ahead. I'm just going to read the Galactic Free Press for a while. Didn't you say that staying current is one of the most important things for a trader?"

"Goodnight," Kevin replied, pulling himself back into his command chair and loosely redoing the harness. He glanced over at the dog bed to make sure Alexander was netted in, and fell asleep within minutes.

The Vergallian equivalent of a saber-toothed tiger chased Kevin through a primordial fern forest. He ran faster and faster, but it seemed like he was stuck on a sheet of ice, and the giant carnivore closed in for the kill. Gasping for breath, Kevin made a desperate leap for an overhead frond, hoping that the giant plant would support his weight and not the tiger's. His hands closed on thin air just short of his target, and he fell back towards the ravenous beast, awakening with a start. The "thump, thump, thump," of running feet was the only sound in the silence of the tunnel.

"I thought you were going to sleep," Dorothy panted, not slowing her pace on the tie-down treadmill. "I feel like a hundred percent better. That beetle is a genius."

"How long have you been on there?"

"I don't know. The display thingy says that I've generated a hundred and thirty-two whelks. What's a whelk?"

"A Sharf energy unit, and take it easy. You're not used to running in Zero-G. It seems easy when you start out because your heart isn't working as hard, but you can overuse your leg muscles without realizing it."

"This is nothing," Dorothy said dismissively. "You know that I can dance for hours. I bet I could out-generate you on any of these machines."

"Bet me what?" Kevin released his safety restraints, pushed off from the back of the chair, and caught himself on the Drazen rock-climbing trainer. The bridge of the converted four-man Sharf scout provided ample space for Zero-G exercise equipment, and Kevin had installed as many machines as he could cram in, unsure of which the girl would like.

"Whoever wins has to do what the other one says without question for a day."

"Deal," he said. "I'm not likely to get back to sleep any time soon, and we should try to stay on the same waking schedule. Are we going to take turns on the treadmill, or do you want to try one of the tandem machines?"

"How about the bicycle with both foot pedals and hand cranks?"

"I don't want you to wear yourself out your first day in space."

"I bike around Mac's Bones all the time. I think you're just chicken."

"A bicycle for two it is, then, but drink some water first."

Dorothy unhooked the elastic tethers from the complex harness that pulled her body towards the track as she ran, while Kevin retrieved two squeeze-tubes of Union Station Springs mineral water from the packaged liquids storage locker. The dog, who had woken from a dream of chasing a giant rabbit during the conversation, wriggled out from under the netting and launched himself at the treadmill.

"What?" Dorothy asked. "Do you want in on the bet?"

Alexander grinned and caught the harness between his teeth, bringing himself to a halt.

"Did you say there's a different harness for the dog, or does this one adapt?" the girl called to Kevin.

"Drink your water, I'll fix him up. The quadruped harness is simpler than the bipedal one since all of the elastics are the same length. I ordered a complete set, even though your dad told me that Cayl hounds don't really need to exercise in Zero-G to stay in shape. Neither do the Cayl, for that matter."

"How is that?"

"Millions of years of breeding and acclimation. Your dad said that they can basically go into hibernation in space and it keeps their muscle tone from deteriorating. But Alex may want to stay awake with us just to make sure we don't have any fun without him."

After Dorothy finished her water and Kevin got the dog strapped down to the treadmill and reset the power counter, the two humans pushed off of various objects of opportunity to reach the tandem exercise bike, which was secured by a fold-out mount to what would be the ceiling of the bridge if the ship was under acceleration.

"You're not feeling any vertigo?" Kevin asked while helping the girl secure herself to the seat and pedals. "Some people have trouble getting used to doing this upside-down."

"It's space, there is no upside-down," she replied loftily. "Stop procrastinating. I'm going to ride you into the ground."

"The bet is for the most power generated in a half-hour," Kevin told her. "I'm not going to let you exhaust yourself while you're hopped up on Farling medicine."

"Let's get started already."

Kevin quickly worked himself into the bicycle harness, placed his feet in the lower pedal stirrups and his hands on the cranks, and said, "Ship. Set timer thirty minutes with ten-minute notifications. Go!" The two of them began pedaling furiously, while below, Alexander started off on the treadmill at an easy lope.

"First notification," the ship announced after ten minutes.

"Are you still feeling okay?" Kevin huffed.

"I'm fine," the girl replied shortly. "Seventy-three whelks."

"Seventy," he grunted back, and picked up the pace.

"Second notification," the ship announced twenty minutes into the competition.

"One fifty-two," Dorothy said.

"One fifty-two," he replied, pedaling harder.

"Stupid arm cranks," the girl panted, taking a brief break and stretching her cramped fingers while she continued pumping with her legs. Then she grabbed hold again and headed for the home stretch.

"Thirty minutes," the ship announced.

"Acknowledge," Kevin said, and ceased pedaling. He leaned out to look over the girl's shoulder and read off of her display the power she had generated for the back-up cells. "Two twenty-four. You were fading at the end."

"I ran before this," Dorothy protested automatically, even while she fought to catch her breath. "What did you get?"

"Two-thirty," Kevin told her. "I guess you'll actually have to listen to the captain for a day now."

"Check how Alexander did first."

Kevin looked up towards the deck and saw that the dog was sprinting along the treadmill, his legs practically a blur. "Hey. Time!" he shouted, and Alexander immediately began easing up, dropping from a bounding run back into a trot.

"If you beat me by like five whelks or something, it doesn't count," Kevin warned the dog, unstrapping himself from the bicycle and repositioning so that he could see the treadmill's screen. "Four hundred and twenty?"

The dog finally came to a halt and looked up, giving his humans a lazy grin.

"Hah!" Dorothy said. "Alexander wins, so the bet is off."

A deep growl rumbled in the dog's chest.

"All right, all right," Kevin said. "But we're not doing anything crazy like rubbing your belly for twenty-four hours straight, or feeding you all of the treats we brought to last the whole trip."

"We could rub his belly in shifts," Dorothy suggested. "I can go first because I'm not sleepy at all."

"That's what I'm worried about. Didn't you get up early this morning?"

"I've stayed up all night at work drinking coffee plenty of times. You know that Affie and Flazint are on different sleep schedules, and sometimes we just needed to push through and get something done."

"What? Like a fashion emergency?"

"Don't laugh, it's a real business. Just because you've been dressing in the same thing every day since you were seven years old doesn't mean that everybody else does. Keeping up with the latest trends and coming up with designs that can be adapted for a dozen different species is a full-time job."

"But you told me that SBJ Fashions was the trendsetter."

"Locally, in cross-species design, but it's not like Union Station exists in a vacuum."

"Uh, actually…"

"It's an expression, and you don't have to point it out every time I make a little mistake," Dorothy retorted. She made her way over to the impatient-looking dog and began scratching behind his ears. "What I mean is that if we design clothes that are too far out, they might look good on a Vergallian model, but nobody will ever buy them. So when we design, like, a new ball gown, it still has to say 'ball gown' to everybody who sees it."

"So you have to keep up with the latest trends to see what the other designers are getting away with?"

"Design is an art form, like painting or writing. Artists learn from each other, push on new boundaries together. It's like the new hat that Fabulous Frunge brought out last year."

"How would their hair vines get enough light?"

"So the previous Frunge hat designs were usually made from transparent materials with a built-in misting system, sort of like a specialty greenhouse, but in miniature."

"Sounds reasonable, I guess."

Dorothy gave him a disgusted look. "Reasonable? Would you want to walk around with a greenhouse on your head?"

"I don't know. Some of the trellis work I've seen on Flazint's head is pretty industrial looking."

"Those are just for training the vines. She substitutes something elegant when she goes out. You just aren't paying attention."

"I guess not," Kevin admitted, his eyelids beginning to droop.

"Frunge don't need hats at all on space stations, though sometimes they wear shade netting if the light spectrum is wrong. I'm talking about hats for fashion here."

"I'm losing track. The new hat that, uh, Fabulous brought out wasn't a greenhouse?"

"No, it was just a brim. Isn't that brilliant?"

"Huh?"

"They eliminated the whole functionality issue through thinking outside of the box. By not covering the head, there's no problem with letting light or moisture through."

"But it's not really a hat then, is it?"

"You have no imagination at all. Of course it's a hat. But Fabulous was, like, it has to be flat and rigid, and being Frunge, they made them out of a light alloy that may as well have been plastic."

"Wait. Do you mean that game the kids were playing last year with the flying disc was…"

"Exactly. The hats were a smash hit with the Frunge until the other species started using them as a toy, and then anybody actually wearing one just looked silly. Fabulous went from a trendsetter to a flop in less than a cycle."

"That doesn't seem fair. It's not that I get why anybody would wear a hollow hat brim to start with, but to have a business wrecked because the other species misused your product is pretty rough."

"Oh, they made a mint selling the hats as flying discs, but nobody takes them seriously in fashion anymore. There's nothing worse than getting laughed at."

"All right, but what does accidentally creating toys have to do with following trends and artists pushing each other?"

"Bite him," Dorothy commanded, turning Alexander's muzzle towards Kevin and pointing. The dog yawned. "Who told you to remember everything I say like some kind of Horten advocate? Living with you is like being constantly on trial."

"I thought you liked it when I asked questions about your work."

"Oh, so you're only pretending to be interested to get on my good side?"

"This isn't like you, Dorothy. You always speak your mind, but you're usually not this argumentative. Are you going to get mad if I suggest taking that Farling patch off of your neck for a while?"

Dorothy clamped her hand over the patch and let out a growl that would have done Beowulf proud.

"Just asking. Still, we might want to cut the next one in half, and maybe try it on your ankle instead."

Alexander barked his agreement.

Six

"Give me the blue five-point, Sam." Joe's legs from the knee down were the only part of him visible because the rest of his body was wedged in under the heat exchanger. "Just slide it in and I'll grab it."

"You should let me do this stuff, Dad," the teen replied, even as he complied with the request. "Vivian says it's inefficient for the most knowledgeable worker on the job to do the grunt work. You're supposed to be promoted to your level of incompetence, and then backed off a fraction, like seating a bearing."

"Wrong blue," his father grunted, and the socket came rolling back out from under the heat exchanger. "I meant the darker one."

"Navy blue?"

"Yeah, that's it. Your old man really is getting old when he can't even tell socket colors anymore."

"The Sharf should size their pentagonal bolts with numbers instead of color shades and then you wouldn't have to guess." Samuel retrieved the socket that had rolled past him, replaced it on the holder strip, and selected its neighbor, which was somewhere between blue and black. Then he squirmed partway under the heat exchanger so he could see what was going on, and placed the socket directly in his father's hand.

"We had numbered sockets on Earth when I was a kid, two different kinds of them. Your grandfather's old pickup used metric sizes on the power train, and what we called 'English' sizes for the body."

"That sounds crazy. How could you tell which was which?"

"If you didn't know the vehicle, you just had to try both and go with the best fit. There were some sizes that were pretty close to being the same thing in both measurement systems, but it was easy to round a bolt by mistake."

"So you needed two sets of ratchet wrenches and everything?"

"No, the drive size was always in inches, rather than millimeters. It might have been different in other countries. Hey, can you hold this copper tube in place?"

"Just a sec." Samuel tried to roll over on his back, but there wasn't enough clearance for his shoulders, so he wriggled out from under the densely packed tubes and then slid back under in the proper orientation. "This one?"

"Thanks." Joe installed the hold-down bolts with his fingers and then used the ratchet wrench to tighten them, alternating back and forth to keep the manifold pressure even. "How are things going at the university?"

"It's different. I mean, you'd think that a course titled 'Introduction to Space Engineering' would include something about either space or engineering, but it's all math. I asked Paul if it was that way when he went, and he said I should just take the competency exam and skip forward as soon as possible."

"Sounds like good advice."

"Yeah, but Libby never gave us tests like that so I'm kind of nervous."

"It seems to me that when I was a kid, all we had in school were tests." Joe put a final torque on the bolts. "Then again, the tests are probably the only thing I remember. How's Ailia doing these days?"

"She's practically a prisoner in her own palace, what with tutors and all," Samuel replied, before the significance of the question hit him. "Wait. You know?"

"Baylit told me a couple of years ago about the linked toy robots that Jeeves set you up with, but I remember how important privacy is to kids."

"Does mom know too?"

"Not unless somebody else spilled the beans. I'm bringing it up now because I figure that you're old enough to understand that we're all part of something bigger, and too many secrets just sets up walls between people. I used to spend a lot of time by myself as a boy, and I remember my father warning me that it's no good going through life alone. I'm glad you didn't take after me."

"But you're not a loner. You even adopted Paul before you got married, and dogs love you."

"I was already on the wrong side of forty when I married your mom, and there are people who would say that dogs don't count."

"Crazy people," Samuel said indignantly. "And you're not mad about me hanging out with Ailia in secret all these years?"

"I might have been worried if you didn't spend so much time with Vivian. She's a great kid. I liked Ailia a lot too when she was with us, but you must have figured out by now that she's not free to do whatever she wants."

"You know that drama I've been watching the last few months? The one with all the good sword-fighting scenes I export to the fencing bot for practice?"

"I had enough of Vergallian culture serving on their worlds, Sam, but I've noticed your sister and Aisha watching with you."

"It's titled, 'Throne of Chains,' and Ailia recommended it. There's a young queen who everybody thinks is on top of the world, but in reality she has less freedom than her least subject. It's pretty sad, and Ailia's been missing more of our meeting times lately because she can't get free."

"Well, I hope that drama exaggerates the situation," Joe said sympathetically. "Let's get out from under here and test for leaks."

Once they were back on their feet, Samuel headed out to fetch Beowulf, and Joe climbed the ladder to the Nova's bridge to manually activate the cooling system. A few minutes later, they met back on the technical deck, where they stood back out of the dog's way.

Beowulf approached the heat exchanger and cocked his head, listening to the circulation of thermal fluids. Then he carefully sniffed all around the base of the unit, at times sprawling on his belly to stick his nose underneath the tubes. Finally, he stretched, shook himself as if he were wet, and broke into a big doggy smile.

"Now what would Vivian say about the most knowledgeable worker on the job?" Joe said, scratching the dog behind the ears.

"Beowulf passed the heat exchanger?" Paul asked, appearing at the top of the Nova's cargo ramp. "I was worried that we'd have to pull the whole thing for a complete rework."

"Dad replaced the filter, cleaned off the catalyst, and changed out a leaky tube," Samuel answered for his father. "You guys have put a lot of hours on her the last couple years."

"Yeah, the catalyst was the real problem," Joe said. "It was covered with some kind of film that prevented it from de-acidifying the condensate. I'm not really sure why it happened, but we probably need to flush the whole system sometime."

"I'll bet the Nova feels like the shoemaker's son, now that we have so many ships to work on," Paul said.

"What's that?" Samuel asked.

"The shoemaker's son always goes barefoot," his father explained. "It's just another way of saying that people who work for others all day don't always have the time or energy to take care of their own."

"Sounds like the answer to one of those word games that mom and Dring are always playing."

"Speaking of which, are you sure you don't want to go on the mission with your mother? It's a once-in-a-lifetime opportunity."

"It's going to be all diplomats and salesmen," Samuel said dismissively. "Besides, the open Vergallian ballroom trials are coming up again, and I'm too busy with school and work to just take off without even knowing how long it will be."

"Jeeves said he expects the whole mission to take less than two weeks, and half of that is just Wylx going slow so the passengers don't suffer from jump sickness," Paul commented.

"I was just mentioning it," Joe said. "I guess that between mom's colleagues and your Stryx friends, neither of you can get too excited about meeting new species."

"Were there really no aliens at all where you grew up?" Samuel asked his father.

"There were barely even any people, Sam. It was just wide open country, a patchwork of cattle ranches and abandoned farms. You have to remember that Earth's population began falling rapidly after the Stryx opened the planet, and by the time I was your age, the world was losing a hundred million people a year. That's a lot of food production that wasn't needed anymore, and most of those farms and ranches barely got by even before the great opening."

"But you still own land on Earth?" Paul asked.

"Nearly a thousand acres," Joe replied. "The local government had long since packed it in, so there weren't any property taxes to pay, which meant nobody had an excuse to take it from me after my parents died. Sam and I visited when we were on Earth last time, but the old house was gutted, and the whole place had pretty much gone back to nature."

"Still, it means we'd have somewhere to land a ship if we ever had a reason," his foster son said with a grin.

"It's something to think about. I know that Kelly wants to get back to visit her mom again now that Marge is no longer traveling."

"I'll come along for that," Samuel said. "When is Aisha going back to work, Paul?"

"A couple more weeks. Who would have thought that the Grenouthians would offer nine months of paid maternity leave? I guess it's just a standard part of their contract for show hosts because Aisha said it never even came up in the negotiations."

"Funny they should have hit on nine months," Joe remarked.

"I never explained it? The bunnies believe that the mother should get time off equal to the length of the pregnancy, so it varies with the species. Her producer told me that they're looking into hiring more human hosts now that they know we're such a bargain. The older the species, the longer it takes to carry a pregnancy to term."

"Didn't you say something about needing to start your homework before supper?" Joe asked Samuel, adding a wink.

"Grains!" the teen swore in kitchen Frunge. "I'll see you later." He tore out of the Nova, running for the ice harvester, with Beowulf charging alongside just for the exercise.

"Ailia?" Paul guessed.

"You know about that too?"

"Jeeves hinted about it a couple of times, and I couldn't help noticing when Aisha and I still lived with you guys that the time Samuel spends alone in his room cycles through a regular pattern. It just made sense that he was accommodating the schedule of somebody on a completely different clock, and Ailia was the only logical guess."

As soon as Samuel reached the ice harvester, he dodged his way through the living room furniture and ran for his bedroom. There he rapidly pulled on his customized flight suit from the Physics Ride and activated his toy robot. A moment later, Ailia stood in front of him, her hologram so solid that it could have fooled anybody in low light.

"Sorry I'm late," the boy apologized. "I was helping my dad with some repairs."

"I kept busy reading," the Vergallian girl replied, setting aside a scroll. "If I could just cut back on the legal studies, I'd have more free time, but I've only got twenty years to get through it all."

"Twenty years! I thought you finished everything early and the new tutors were all for electives."

"There's no such thing as elections in the empire," she joked, intentionally misunderstanding him. Unlike Vergallian, English had no built-in error correction mechanisms to prevent listeners from mishearing words that began with the same sounds. "Baylit said that to be respected as a queen, I at least need to master the basics of jurisprudence, economic management, and diplomacy."

"But twenty years. We'll be thirty-six by the time you're queen."

"Twenty years is just for the law. Baylit has promised to continue as regent until I'm at least fifty, but I'm hoping she'll stay on a couple of decades longer. Being queen isn't just who you are and what you've studied. Nobody will take me seriously before I'm old enough to marry."

"You're talking about starting life at the age most humans retire," Samuel grumbled.

"But you've always known that," Ailia said, smiling at his boyish irritability over things that couldn't be changed. "Give me your hand. I've learned a whole new set of steps to 'Unending Glory,' and we'd better get started if you're going to have time to teach them to Vivian before the trials."

For the next fifty minutes, Samuel danced around his room with Ailia, the modified flying suit providing tactile feedback so lifelike that he could forget that his partner was a hologram when he closed his eyes.

"You learn faster than any of the Vergallian boys in the dance class," Ailia complimented him after a flawless performance. "It's too bad..." The girl trailed off and looked away, but not before Samuel noticed the sadness around her eyes.

"What's wrong? Are the borderlands making trouble again?"

"Those barbarians? Baylit could run them off the planet with one arm tied behind her back."

68

"Is it because your schedule is so packed? If you want to change times, I can always swap with somebody at the lost-and-found, or I can just work with Dad and Paul to pay the Open University fees. It's not a big deal."

"That's not it. Besides, you said that the lost-and-found job is ideal for studying because hardly anybody comes in. It's nothing, really."

"Did you get another betrothal offer?" Samuel asked sharply. The girl didn't respond, but she refused to meet his eyes. "That's crazy. You can't even get married for another forty years and they're trying to tie you to some kid you've never met."

"My family's world is a freehold," Ailia reminded him. "Most of the planets in the empire are imperial grants, but our ancestors built this place up on their own and only chose to join later. We don't have a seat on the council, but they don't have the right to tax us. There are plenty of wealthy Vergallians who would pay almost any price to be able to use us as a tax shelter. It's one of the reasons my family was killed through treachery in the first place."

"Just because some rich aliens want a tax shelter is no reason for you to marry their stupid son!"

"They aren't aliens to me, Sam, but there's nothing they can offer us that we need. Baylit says we have to go through the motions, though, or we'll just pile up enemies. Vergallians respect a woman's right to reject a suitor for any reason, but if we don't at least entertain reasonable offers, we'll offend their honor."

"Reasonable offers? You mean there's some kind of litmus test for who has a right to harass you?"

Ailia couldn't help laughing at her friend's distress, and her dark mood passed. "It's not harassment, Sam. It's politics. I'm beginning to wonder what they teach in Vergallian Studies at your Open University."

"We haven't gotten to any of the good stuff yet," he admitted. "It's all imperial history so far, and you guys have been around so long that there's way too much of it. I know some kids from the station who major in Human Studies and they just party all the time. Watch a few Grenouthian documentaries and you know it all."

"I'm sure there's more to Human history than that, Sam. What's Vivian majoring in?"

"Dynastic Studies. She's like the only human taking it."

"It must be hard for her," Ailia sympathized.

"She's not even fifteen yet, but you'd think she was a grownup," Samuel said. "She says I should add three years to her age because girls mature faster than boys, and everybody else says I should add ten years to her age for being Blythe's daughter."

"The poor girl will be an old maid before she's sixteen if you keep piling on the years like that. Doesn't she have a twin brother?"

"Jonah. He's cool, but I don't see much of him anymore. He wanted to take a break from school before university, so he works for InstaSitter part-time, and he's doing an internship at EarthCent Intelligence."

"Strong family, they sound like Vergallians," Ailia said approvingly. "Is she pretty, your Vivian?"

"Not like you," Samuel blurted. "And we're just friends, you know. She's only a little kid."

"I thought you told me she was practically twenty-five."

"I was repeating what other people say. I mean, she's really good at dancing and fencing, and she got through Libby's school like two years faster than me, but I'm a head taller than her."

"And whatever happened to Banger?" Ailia asked, referring to the little Stryx who was Samuel's work/play assignment. She had made friends with Banger during the six months she lived with the McAllisters after being abandoned by her nurse on the set of 'Let's Make Friends.'

"I haven't seen him in over a year. I guess he's busy exploring the multiverse, and Jeeves told me that it's easy for Stryx to forget how quickly time passes for humans. Banger might get caught up working on some math puzzle, and by the time he figures it out, we'll all be dead."

"I'm sure he'd come if you asked Jeeves to call him."

"I would if I had more time to spend with him, but it wouldn't be right to invite him to come visit, and then only have a couple of hours a day to hang out."

"I hope you aren't neglecting Vivian when you aren't practicing your ballroom dancing."

"Oh, I see her every day at the university too. We usually eat lunch together, and sometimes she comes by the lost-and-found and does homework with me. And we fence at least once a week, though she cheats."

"Cheats?"

"You know, she won't fight by Vergallian rules."

"That's very wise of her," Ailia said softly.

"She's really a lot of fun," Samuel continued. "I wish you could meet her. I think the two of you would be great friends."

Seven

Kelly tried to weave her way through the crowd of around two dozen people blocking the entrance to the EarthCent embassy. She was carrying a flat box containing a half-dozen donuts from Hole Universe in honor of Friday, and she was afraid they would get crushed. The ambassador momentarily regretted her decision to stop wearing heels when she turned fifty-five because she couldn't see over any of the men in front of her, but then she heard Donna's voice above the loud conversations.

"None of you are getting first dibs on the ambassador if you don't get out of her way," the embassy manager warned the crowd. "Everybody just squeeze over to your right and open a path for her."

The threat did the trick, and amidst a good deal of grumbling a narrow passage opened to Kelly's left, and she brought the donuts safely through to the reception desk.

"Libby told me you were stuck outside," Donna explained. "After Daniel announced to his Sovereign Human Communities group that you had authorization to include a trade delegation on the mission, they all made record time getting here."

"I didn't bring enough for everybody," Kelly whispered in dismay. "We can't just eat in front of them."

"Don't worry, they'll all be out of here soon. Daniel's organization has a budget for meeting space. When I pinged him at home about the turnout, he headed for the Little Apple to help Ian get Pub Haggis open. They don't usually serve breakfast."

"Good move. But why are all of the people still here?"

"Ian asked me to wait until they prepared the restaurant for business. It's tough to get the chairs down and the tables moved into place if it's packed with people." Donna stopped and pointed at her ear to let Kelly know that she had an incoming message. Then she nodded and announced in a loud voice, "Associate Ambassador Cohan has arranged to meet you all at Pub Haggis in the Little Apple. Seating is on a first-come, first-serve basis, and Ambassador McAllister will follow you there."

There was an immediate stampede for the lift tubes in the corridor. The jam cleared in less than two minutes, though the early arrivals who had been inside the embassy at the front of the line complained loudly about the unfairness of the whole process.

"That was just a little mean," Kelly observed. "You know that Pub Haggis has more than enough space for everybody."

Donna shrugged. "I'm the one who sent out Daniel's announcement. The recipients were supposed to contact us for individual meetings, but they all tried to get a jump on each other by showing up here."

"Oh. Well, now we have too many donuts," Kelly said, then clamped her hand over her mouth in disbelief that she had uttered such blasphemy. Donna opened the box and removed a honey-dipped, and then the ambassador took a triple-chocolate and bit into it with a sigh. "Daniel usually eats three."

"Don't talk with your mouth full. Daniel won't turn his nose up at slightly stale donuts when he gets back here, and I'll put one aside for Lynx."

"I could manage another half," the ambassador said hopefully, but her friend folded the tabs of the box back into place and set it out of Kelly's reach. "Anyway, did you just commit me to going to Pub Haggis?"

"You may as well participate in picking the lucky winners since you're going to be traveling with them," Donna pointed out. "Libby. How many extra people can Kelly bring along?"

"There isn't a hard limit on the size of the delegation, but you wouldn't want to overwhelm the Alts. It's up to the ambassador to decide, though I might suggest making selections that will reflect positively on humanity's integration with the tunnel network."

"Letting us off of probation would be a positive reflection," Kelly hinted, but the Stryx librarian didn't rise to the bait. "So you mean I should bring along a representative from the open worlds of each different species rather than pushing for commercial ties right off?"

"Excellent decision," Libby confirmed. "Especially since you have no way of knowing what products might be of interest to the Alts."

"Sounds like a plan," Donna said. "Pushing for business before we've even established relations or persuaded them to join the tunnel network would be putting the cart before the horse. By the way, Chastity wants to talk to you about press coverage."

"Oh, so now you want a favor," Kelly drawled, eyeing the forbidden donuts. "You know, what with running back and forth to Ian's and arguing with a bunch of businessmen who won't like being left behind, I'll be burning off plenty of extra calories today."

"Half," Donna grudgingly agreed, reopening the donut box and breaking the other triple chocolate donut into two pieces. She offered the smaller half to Kelly, who displayed her negotiating skill by merely lifting an eyebrow. "It's your funeral," the embassy manager warned, giving in and passing over the larger piece.

"I was going to invite Chastity anyway," the ambassador taunted, dancing back out of Donna's reach. With the partially eaten donut in one hand and the newly divided half in the other, she looked every inch the chocoholic that she was.

"Chastity wants to bring one reporter from Union Station and two Children's News Network correspondents from Earth."

"The kids from Earth were the president's idea," Kelly said. "I guess a local reporter won't hurt anything, and the press will help keep the alien ambassadors and Daniel's people out of my hair."

"You better head down there before he tells them they can all go along to get them out of *his* hair," Donna advised.

"Good point," the ambassador mumbled with her mouth full, and headed for the corridor. "I'll be back."

"I'm pinging Ian and telling him not to let you have anything to eat," Donna called after her. "And you just lost your gold star for the day on our diet chart."

Kelly sucked the chocolate off the fingers of her free hand before turning her attention to the bonus half. She walked rapidly towards the Little Apple, though she was sorely tempted to take the lift tube to save the fifteen minutes. The ambassador compromised by pinging Daniel and asking him not to make any promises before she arrived.

By the time Kelly walked into Pub Haggis, Ian was refilling the giant urn of coffee, and most of the would-be representatives for the scattered human communities were giving their full attention to a Scottish breakfast.

"Ian," Kelly greeted the proprietor, who she hadn't seen in several months. "Thank you for accommodating us on such short notice."

"Coffee or tea only," he told her by way of a reply. "Orders from the boss."

"I was just headed for the tea selection," Kelly fibbed, skipping past the breakfast pastries that Ian must have ordered in from elsewhere. "Have I missed any speeches?"

"Daniel told everybody to order breakfast and wait until you got here. Interesting bunch of people he's collected."

While letting her tea bag steep in the mug of hot water, the ambassador took a minute to study the group of candidates for her mission, and found that she had to agree with Ian's assessment. It was clear that they were all dressed to impress, but something about their choice of formalwear was just a little off. She saw one fellow in a custom tailored suit with what looked like a leather axe holder protruding from a reinforced patch on the shoulder, and a woman in a green lamé dress that would have been perfect on a mermaid.

Daniel approached the hot drinks station to refill his coffee and greeted the ambassador. "I hope you saved me some donuts. I didn't forget that it was your turn to buy this Friday."

"Donna put them in your office. How did you choose who to invite for today?"

"I used population for a cut-off, so everybody here represents a sovereign community with at least a million members, though we count all of the factory towns or mines on open worlds as a single community. These people are professional travelers who keep a go-bag at the office, and their worlds are all on the tunnel network, so I'm not surprised they made it so fast."

"They're dressed a bit—funny."

"Really? I didn't notice."

"Well, what about the guy with the parasol?"

"Dirk Henshaw, though he prefers to be called 'Dyhenth' these days. He's from a community specializing in materials engineering on a Verlock open world. The planet is much closer to its sun than most places humans would choose to live, so parasols and pith helmets are pretty much required."

"And the mermaid?"

"Suzy. She doesn't use a last name any more. Suzy represents several of our communities on the oldest Frunge open world. Many of the humans who used to work as laborers in metallic fabric manufacturing there stayed after their contract expirations to start their own specialty mills. That dress may look slinky, but it's proof against most handheld projectile weapons, though unless you wore heavy padding underneath, you'd end up with a magnificent bruise."

"I see. What's with the people at the table in the corner where everybody is wearing hoodies that look like they could double as straitjackets?"

Daniel shrugged. "It's the latest fashion with humans on some Dollnick worlds. I guess they're trying to compensate for only having two arms by sewing those empty sleeves across the front. Makes as much sense as any fashion, I guess, but don't tell Shaina you heard me say that."

"It's a good thing the Hortens don't have many open worlds or your members would be covering themselves in make-up," Kelly jested. She saw the associate ambassador wince as he stared over her shoulder, and she turned to see a woman with a fire-engine red face. "Oops."

"Ursula," the newcomer said shortly. "From Horten Forty-Six, their first open world."

"I'm so sorry," Kelly apologized, noting that the bright red of the woman's complexion was fading rapidly to pink before her eyes. "How do you do that?"

"My thermal makeup? It uses nanobot technology licensed from the Gem to integrate and amplify changes in skin temperature and perspiration and then alter the displayed color accordingly."

"I guess it comes in handy if you're living on a Horten world," Kelly said diplomatically.

"Actually, it's beginning to sell very well in boutiques throughout the station network. 'Honesty' is the brand name. I'm sure that the Alts will be very enthusiastic about it," Ursula concluded, her face taking on a light brown shade that could have been mistaken for a tan. "It also moisturizes and offers better protection from ultraviolet radiation than standard sunblockers."

"Do you have samples?" inquired the man in the pith helmet, who had joined the group which was forming around the hot drink urns.

Ursula delved into her over-sized purse and came up with a handful of plasticized rectangular packages that reminded Kelly of the condiment packets that came with take-out food. "Just remember," she cautioned, counting five samples into Dyhenth's hands. "Your face will be an open book, so don't get in a poker game or try fibbing to your wife."

"Thanks. I'm not married, actually."

"Excuse me, Ambassador McAllister," somebody said at Kelly's elbow, tearing her attention away from the colorful pair. "I noticed you looking at my dress earlier, and I was wondering if I could get a meeting…"

"We're going to try to settle on the delegation right here so that we don't keep any of you from your work longer than necessary," Kelly cut her off. "Do you know if you're the only candidate from a Frunge open world here today?"

"I believe so, yes, but you didn't let me finish. I was hoping you could introduce me to your daughter. You are Dorothy McAllister's mother, aren't you?"

"Yes, I—my daughter?"

"The fashion designer," Suzy said patiently, as if she were talking to a child. "We have an exciting new line of metallic fabrics produced with Frunge techniques that I'm sure she would find of interest."

"I'm sorry I misunderstood. I've sort of lost my ability to multi-task as I've gotten older," Kelly apologized. "I'm afraid Dorothy left Union Station last week on an extended trip. I know that SBJ Fashions is always open to new ideas, and I'm sure Associate Ambassador Cohan will be glad to introduce you to his wife, who is one of the partners."

"Shaina or Brinda?" asked the fabric rep, who had obviously done her homework.

"Shaina," Kelly replied. "I think she uses her maiden name at work."

"Shaina Hadad," Suzy affirmed. "She's married to Daniel Cohan? I mean, if you people are going to persist in using multiple names, you could at least be consistent about it."

"My feeling exactly," Daniel said, turning back to the conversation after hearing his name. "Feel free to bring it up with her. My son, Michael Hadad-Cohan, will thank you." He blew on his second coffee, took a sip, and then addressed Kelly. "We may as well get started while everybody is in a good mood from the food."

The ambassador nodded and moved towards the section of the buffet where Ian had optimistically set out a haggis, leading to an open space in front of the table. Daniel came along with her, quietly discouraging the sales reps from following, and the conversations at the tables died out as everybody returned to their seats.

"Good morning," Kelly began. "I am Ambassador McAllister and I've been asked by the Stryx to lead the, uh, biological contingent of the upcoming mission to the Alts. I'm sure you all know as much as I do about it from reading the Galactic Free Press, so let me get right to the point. While business is a large component of any relationship between species, for a first contact mission, we want to emphasize the benefits of trade as opposed to closing deals."

"There is no benefit unless you close deals," somebody called out.

"Yes, I'm aware of that. But you have to keep in mind that none of us have a clue what this new species might be like or what products would interest them. What we hope to accomplish, with your cooperation, is to show how humanity has quickly adapted some of the products and technologies of alien species, and in that way, to encourage the Alts to do the same."

"You want to invite them to compete with us?" a woman asked incredulously. "Where's the profit in that?"

"We're not here to discuss making money today, Pinka," Daniel addressed the woman, who was wearing a gold-plated Drazen pitch pipe on a necklace. "This is a Stryx mission and we're just along to make a good impression. Think of it as an honor."

"I've been told by several of my colleagues from other species that unless the Alts reject the Stryx outright, we should expect a large delegation of them to accompany us back to Union Station to see what the tunnel network is all about," Kelly continued. "I'm sure that some of you have seen the announcements for the Dollnick resort worlds trade show that will be monopolizing the Empire Convention Center starting this weekend and running through the next two cycles. They have graciously agreed to vacate part of the Nebula room for an all-species commerce show on being notified that an Alt delegation is returning with us."

"So the smart move is staying here and preparing," Pinka concluded.

"Better to spread our chances," said the man with the axe-loop. "Why doesn't each community send a representative to make a good impression, and the rest of us can work on getting ready for a show?"

"Can we agree right now that any information about the new customers sent back by representatives on the mission is shared among all of us?" another man asked.

"Agreed," practically the whole room chorused.

"I'll go," Suzy volunteered. "There's plenty of time for one of our other reps to get here and handle the setup."

"Count me in," Dyhenth said, winking at the brown-faced woman who had accompanied him back to the table of reps from Verlock open worlds.

"Me too," Ursula chimed in.

"That covers the Frunge, the Verlocks and the Hortens," Daniel said. "Who's going to represent a Dollnick world?"

"I'll do it," Bob offered. "Our floaters sell themselves in any case."

"Come on, which of you axe-wielders is going to step up," the associate ambassador challenged the humans from Drazen open worlds.

"I guess I can do it," the woman with the gold pitch pipe said, drawing a round of applause for being a good sport.

"Don't you have somebody from a Vergallian world?" Kelly asked Daniel.

"Not a sovereign community, the Empire doesn't work that way," he replied. "Am I leaving anybody out?"

"Five is perfect," Kelly declared. "The current plan has us leaving Sunday evening, so you have two days to take care of any other business you may have on the station. Please enjoy your breakfasts, and if you have any questions, just ask the station librarian and she'll get a message to me if it's necessary."

"Thank you for volunteering me," Libby said privately over the ambassador's implant. "Please accompany the candidates to the Farling medical shop for a health inspection. It won't take more than a few minutes."

"One more thing," Kelly called out as some of the people began rising from their seats for second or third helpings. "The Stryx have arranged for a physician to check the people who are making the trip, I suppose to see if we need any inoculations and such. Will the five of you come along with me and we'll get this over with?"

All of the open-worlds reps were old road warriors, so there was no grumbling over the possibility of being poked by needles. The rest of the crowd remained behind to drink coffee and discuss plans for the trade show as Kelly led her group to the lift tube bank. A minute later they emerged on the travel concourse, not far from the Farling's medical shop.

"Just a word of warning," the ambassador said to the reps. No stranger to showing groups around the station, she walked backwards in front of the five volunteers as they approached the small storefront. "The doctor's bedside manner may leave something to be desired."

"Uh, Ambassador?" Ursula said, motioning with her chin. Kelly turned and saw the beetle, who must have been alerted by Libby, standing in the doorway of his shop.

"I heard that," the Farling rubbed out on his speaking legs.

"I can't believe I've done the same thing twice in one day," the ambassador muttered to herself. "I should learn to keep my mouth shut."

"An unlikely development at your advanced age," M793qK commented. "This will only take a moment if you can all pretend to be members of a moderately intelligent species. Follow me in one at a time so that the entrance scanners have a chance to recover from your vital statistics, and I'll need a blood sample from each of you."

Kelly hung back, allowing Suzy to enter the shop first, and the rep from the Frunge open world emerged less than a minute later, looking rather pleased about something.

"What did he do to you?" the ambassador asked, as the next in line entered the Farling's shop.

"He said I'm very clean and healthy for a human, and he complimented me on the color of my dress."

"Oh. I'll see you Sunday, then."

The next three reps all gave Kelly similar reports as they emerged, and Dyhenth was laughing so hard when he came out that he couldn't talk right away.

"Did he give you something?" the ambassador asked suspiciously.

"A clean bill of health. The doctor has lived on a number of Verlock worlds and his impersonation of them is uncanny. He's waiting for you, now."

"For me? Libby?"

"It's just a formality," the Stryx librarian replied soothingly.

Kelly gazed longingly after Dyhenth as he headed off towards the lift tubes and then reluctantly entered the medical shop. A number of alarms sounded as she passed through the scanner bank.

"Oh, dear," the Farling said. "This won't do at all."

"I hate needles," Kelly pleaded. "I know my inoculations aren't all up to date, but I'll take my chances."

"Your inoculations? I see you've mistaken the purpose of this visit, Ambassador. My job is to protect the Alts from the introduction of foreign diseases."

"I don't have any diseases," Kelly asserted, but her confidence in that statement wilted under the impartial stare of the insect's multi-faceted eyes, "Do I?"

"If I had enough limbs to count up the contagions you're incubating, I'd be a centipede," the beetle retorted. He opened and shut several drawers, looking for some rarely used instrument, and finally came up with a device that reminded Kelly of two halves of a plaster mold connected by a hinge. "Ankle," the Farling commanded.

"What is that?" Kelly asked, backing away. "Am I some kind of paroled convict or something?"

"You lack the education to understand its function, but you can think of it as a sterilization envelope generator. While it's on your ankle, none of the pathogens brewing away within your mortal coil will survive beyond your skin."

"Did you put one of those on everybody?"

"Of course not. Having been born to parents working on alien worlds, there was nothing wrong with any of them. You, on the other hand, must have grown up on your Earth, and I suspect you had the habit of touching things and rubbing your eyes. Between the highly evolved bacteria and viruses of your world, and the primitive state of your medical technology, it's a wonder that any of you ever reached your full height."

"Libby? Do I have to?" Kelly asked out loud.

"You won't feel a thing," the station librarian reassured her.

"Ankle," the doctor demanded again. The ambassador gave in, sitting down on the chair next to the machine that combined a Stryx register with a genetic sequencer, and allowed the insect to snap the bracelet shut on her ankle. "Come see me when you return and I'll remove it."

"Shouldn't I be worried about any of these alleged pathogens, you know, making me sick or anything?"

"Your body has long since adjusted to their presence, which is why I'm loathe to remove them. As it is, you may notice a small side effect to your digestive system, for which I prescribe yogurt."

"But how could my diseases make an alien sick? I thought we were all too different for that."

"The Stryx gave me a list of organisms to screen for and you hit the jackpot," M793qK informed her. "If the mission was planned to reach the planet's surface, I would have advised against your participation as being too high-risk, but I understand that it will take place in orbit. In case of damage to the sterilization device, Stryx Wylx can always decontaminate any Alts you infect before returning them to their world."

"I can't believe Lynx likes you," Kelly said angrily. "You're the worst doctor I've ever met. I think having a baby must have scrambled her brains."

"I expect that I'm the first real doctor you've ever met, if you're going to start making comparisons. I might also point out that your cultural attaché just entered my shop and is standing right behind you."

Eight

"That station is the crowning achievement of Drazen engineering? The Dollnicks build bigger colony ships!"

"Don't let any Drazens hear you say that, Dorothy, and concentric donut stations are notoriously difficult to design. You're going to find that all of the artificial constructs in the galaxy are a bit of a letdown after living on a Stryx station."

"Is the docking hub at Zero-G, then? I was looking forward to getting back to gravity as soon as possible."

"You'll appreciate weightlessness more when you help me unload the cargo. Just remember…"

"I know," she cut him off. "Mass doesn't vanish with weight. Dad drilled that into me when I was a kid. What's with all the dinging and flashing lights?"

"Time to slave the controller," Kevin said, flipping the protective guard off of the sole mechanical switch on the command console and thumbing the rocker into the 'remote' position. "It's not like visiting Union Station where Gryph handles the nearby traffic with manipulator fields and all that the incoming ships have to do is shut down their engines. Every alien station on the tunnel network I've ever visited demands remote access to your ship controller to perform the docking sequence. Can't say that I blame them, considering what's at stake."

"Have you ever been here before?"

"Five or six times at least. I trade at Drazen stations and colonies whenever possible because they like trying new things and it's not that hard to read their body language. There were times I went through my whole inventory trying to find a gadget that would interest a Frunge, but you can always swap half of an uneaten sandwich to a Drazen and get something in return."

"I used to have a Drazen babysitter before she got promoted into management. What are the other main species on this station?"

"There are usually some alien merchants or tourists, but I doubt they come to one percent of the population."

"No decks for different atmosphere mixes?"

"The Stryx are the only ones who go out of their way to support mixed populations. This is a Drazen station. It's basically a supply hub and connection point for their ships in this sector."

"That doesn't sound very interesting. You mean that everybody living on it is basically a warehouse employee or works for a transportation company?"

"There are at least a million inhabitants, so you're talking about schools, restaurants, everything that they need to live comfortably. But it's nowhere near as spacious as the stations and orbitals built by the older species, so the Drazens who live here are usually on contract, rather than a permanent posting. It's just more comfortable for most biologicals to live on a planet."

"So what happens when we arrive?"

"Normally I'd unload enough trade goods to get started and head for the market, but I thought I'd take you on a quick tour first. And there are a few places on the retail corridor that have pretty good synthesizers if you want a break from ship rations."

"Why would I want a break from eating out of squeeze tubes? I especially like the raspberry cheesecake."

"Yeah, that one's pretty bad. I guess that's why Alexander went into hibernation after bossing us around for a day."

"Shouldn't we wake him?"

"May as well wait until we're ready to lay out the blanket," Kevin replied, using trader slang for setting up to trade. "That reminds me of the time I visited one of these stations where there were twice as many dogs as Drazens, and you know that their native canines are a bit hard of hearing…"

By the time the story reached its inevitable punchline, the traffic controller had successfully docked Kevin's converted Sharf scout ship on an airlock stub. The hub was spinning just fast enough to give the new arrivals a sense of up and down, but not much more. The two humans unbuckled their restraints and launched themselves for the hatch. After days in true Zero-G, Dorothy failed to account for her slight increase in weight and had to reach up to grab the handhold. Kevin checked the safety panel for the atmospheric status of the docking lock, nodded, and opened the hatch.

"Fresh air," Dorothy said, inhaling deeply. "I didn't realize how stale it was in the ship."

"The Drazens run a higher oxygen content then we're used to," Kevin cautioned her. "I usually put in my nose plugs when I'm trading because I don't want to get too euphoric."

"I think it's perfect."

"Activate your magnetic cleats. Anywhere you see parallel lines in low-gravity, like the green and red ones here, it means that's the deck and they expect visitors to stay on it."

"Does this passage lead to a lift tube? Why two different colors?"

Kevin shrugged. "We have to go through customs first."

"What do you mean? They're going to give us a test to make sure that we understand Drazen customs? I never thought they were so sensitive about that stuff."

"Some species forbid certain imports and tax others, and on Drazen stations, you also need permission if you're going to work or trade while visiting. It's all handled by the customs agents here, but other species have as many as four levels of officials to get past. The Verlocks don't have any controls, so you just walk through like a Stryx station."

"I was just kidding, of course I know about customs," Dorothy said in exasperation. "You're so literal. And the Stryx do forbid some dangerous imports."

"And since the vast majority of visitors are smart enough not to try to smuggle them onto a Stryx station, there's no need for customs agents. Whatever you do, never admit to having any cash or they'll want a gratuity."

"Aliens asking for bribes? I'm shocked."

"Shhh. It's only their dogs that are hard of hearing," Kevin cautioned her as they queued up in the shortest line. "Ease up on the sarcasm and let me do the talking."

"Next," the customs inspector announced, and Dorothy's high quality implant perfectly translated the boredom in the Drazen's voice. He didn't even look up until the pair reached the turnstile, but then his face split into a wide grin. "Humans! This is my lucky day."

"Uh, thank you," Kevin said. "We're here…"

"Do the song," the customs agent demanded. "Come on, don't be shy."

"The song?"

"The Human song. You know." The inspector lifted the whistle hanging around his neck to his lips and blew a short note. "Hey, everybody. I finally got some new Humans."

"Do the song," another inspector called, and the other officials in the large hall abandoned their posts to gather around.

"I really don't know what you're talking about," Kevin said. "Even if I did know, I don't have much of a singing voice."

"Of course not, you're Human. That's half of the fun. Make it a duet."

Dorothy looked to Kevin for a lead, but he was just standing with his mouth open, so she decided to get it over with and started in on the theme to 'Let's Make Friends.'

Don't be a stranger because I look funny
You look weird to me…

"Not that one," the Drazen interrupted her. "The one about getting sick from hot sauce."

"I'm afraid I don't know it," Dorothy said.

"Hey, what is this?" Kevin demanded. "We're traders from a tunnel network species with treaty rights to…"

"Traders?" the customs inspector cut him off in a disappointed voice. The gathered officials shook their heads and returned to their posts, where the queues were now empty since the other arrivals had all taken advantage of the situation to hop the turnstiles. "Sorry. I assumed you were the latest batch of trainees. Married?"

"No," Dorothy replied a little too quickly.

"I thought you might be siblings with that weird orange hair," the inspector said. "Where are your goods?"

"I'm taking her for a look around the station, and I want to see what the other traders are pushing before we set up," Kevin answered. "And we're not siblings."

"Cousins?" the customs agent guessed.

"We're just traveling together," Dorothy said.

The Drazen held up a hand like a crossing guard stopping pedestrians. "This is a family station. We don't put up with that sort of thing from visitors."

"What are you talking about? The Drazens back on Union Station..."

"This isn't Union Station," the inspector replied shortly. "Entry denied."

"We have a companionship contract," Kevin told him. "It's back on the ship because it's Frunge, so it's a hassle to carry around."

"Why didn't you say so to start with?" The inspector gave them a disgusted look for wasting his time and causing a false alarm. "Any currency to declare?"

"None," the humans answered simultaneously.

"Next," the inspector continued in a bored voice, waving them through the turnstile.

"What was that all about?" Dorothy asked, as they moved down the passage toward one of the spokes.

"Never had anything like that happen in all of my travels, but then I was always by myself," Kevin admitted. He steered her past the first lift tube and continued towards the next spoke. "That last one was for the residential ring. We want the commercial district."

"You remember from being here before?"

"They're labeled in a dozen languages," he pointed out. "You don't read any of them?"

"I never needed to. Which ones can you read?"

"I'm not fluent in anything, but I can figure out basic navigation signage and numbers for most of the tunnel network species. Remember, I had lots of time to kill travelling alone. Hurry up. These things don't run as frequently as on a Stryx station."

They made it into the lift tube just before the doors closed, and imitated the other occupants by shuffling up the wall so that their feet were pointing in the direction of travel. As the capsule moved out the spoke towards the donut ring, their weight slowly increased, and by the time the door slid open five minutes later, they had turned off their magnetic cleats and were able to walk onto the commercial deck.

"All that exercise really paid off," Dorothy said. "I've never felt so strong."

"You're at maybe eighty percent of your weight on Union Station, and don't forget the higher oxygen content in the air."

"Spoilsport. Hey, that smells pretty good."

"Drazen cooking always smells good, but their food contains lots of molecules that humans never encountered on Earth, so our bodies don't realize they're dangerous. Someday I'll remember to ask your station librarian why it doesn't smell bad, though she'll probably tell me that it's competitive information. Where's your EarthCent Intelligence poison detector ring?"

"It doesn't go with this outfit, I'll just watch yours." She frowned. "Do you hear somebody singing in English?"

Kevin gave the silent command to turn off his translation implant and listened intently for a moment. "Yeah, but it doesn't make any sense. I think it's coming from that way."

The two humans headed up the broad corridor, the deck of which was curved so gently that it was only noticeable when looking far ahead. Most of the retail space in this section of the donut was taken by restaurants, which displayed their signage Drazen-style, with polarized holograms that showed different images as the viewing angle changed. Dorothy couldn't make anything of the Drazen script that was usually squeezed between enticing if fanciful representations of the entrees. Then the singing began again, and this time it came from just the other side of a dense crowd of Drazens who blocked their view of the restaurant's entrance.

Hold the seaweed, add the hot sauce
We can't eat it, but that's our loss
Don't forget the free roll of floss
Human Burger

"Look," Dorothy exclaimed as the overhead hologram began flashing 'Human Burger,' in English. "And you said that we wouldn't be able to eat anything other than synthesized food."

"That wasn't here last time I came," Kevin said, obviously surprised by the appearance of a human restaurant on the Drazen station. "It looks like a chain outfit, but I've never heard of them."

It took almost twenty minutes for the couple to reach the counter due to the number of Drazens ordering. There seemed to be an infinite number of variations to the song, depending on the entree chosen by the diners, though all of them concluded with the name of the restaurant. The employees wore puffy collars and round caps, giving the impression that their faces were the filling for a bun.

"Human Burger. How can I help you?" a pert young lady asked Dorothy.

"I'll have a burger I guess, but without any of the dangerous stuff."

The employee did a double-take on hearing Dorothy speak English, and said, "We don't serve humans."

"What? It's in the name of your restaurant!"

"It's not my restaurant, I work for Eccentric Enterprises. And didn't you listen to the song? We really can't eat it."

"That's why I'm saying to just make it plain," Dorothy repeated. "I haven't had any real food in a week."

"I'm sorry, but it's not a regular hamburger with funky condiments. The patty is from vat-grown Mafletzet, which is some sort of giant alien snake, and the flour includes ground glass, which the Drazens hold in their gizzards to soften up indigestible fiber."

"But it smells so good," Dorothy pleaded. "How about an order of fries?"

"We don't get potatoes out here. The fries are from a Drazen tuber that's so poisonous we need regular inoculations of antidote just to work here. They didn't tell us that back on Earth," the girl added ruefully.

"A soda?"

"Not if you want to keep your teeth. The only thing on the menu that any of us can eat is the fruit salad, which we get in 55-gallon drums from Earth."

"How is it?" Kevin asked over Dorothy's shoulder.

"It comes in 55-gallon drums from Earth," the girl repeated, making a face. "The Drazens cover it with hot sauce until it floats, and I don't blame them."

"Two orders of fruit salad," Dorothy said dejectedly.

Hold the burger, hold the bun
Human diets are no fun
Eat like that, you'll lose a ton
Human Burger

"Did you just make that up?" Kevin asked the girl.

"The job interview was all rhyming and singing. I actually thought I was applying for summer stock theatre," she confessed. "But it's good experience for improv, they'll pay for college if I can find one to attend, and there's profit sharing if I last out the contract. The fruit salad will be four creds, by the way."

"I've got this," Dorothy said, and paid the girl.

Immediately after the coins hit the register drawer, one of the cooks behind the grill line dinged a bell and announced, "Two baby foods."

The counter girl retrieved the two bowls, put them on a tray, and slid it across the counter, where Kevin picked it up.

"Human Special with the works," an impatient Drazen behind the couple barked.

Buns that crunch 'cause they're full of glass
All the good stuff, we give a pass
Drazen food knocks me on my—butt
Human Burger

"I could never work here," Dorothy said as she followed Kevin to a table. "Not being able to eat all that great-smelling food."

"I couldn't handle the singing and rhyming. At least now we know what the guy in customs was on about."

"Ugh. How can anything be so tasteless after a week of eating Zero-G rations?"

"At least it's not a paste. I wonder what these bright red waxy things are, though."

"I think they're supposed to be cherries. At least the yellow wedges have substance to them."

"Pineapple?"

"No, I don't think so," Dorothy said, chewing contemplatively.

"Mango?" Kevin suggested after another bite.

"You're just guessing now. I think they might have been cling peaches once."

"Finish up and I'll take you to a synthesizer place I remember. It's really not bad if you put enough salt on it."

"Excuse me," said a Drazen woman, approaching their table with a heavily loaded tray and three children in tow. "Are these seats taken?"

"Please." Kevin added the universal gesture for 'help yourself,' even though the alien must have had an implant programmed for English to understand the girl at the counter.

"Thank you," the woman replied, and said to her children, "Sit, they won't bite you."

"They can't bite us," her oldest boy replied bravely, taking the chair next to Kevin. "We're poison to them."

"Are not," his younger sister insisted. "I'm sweet."

"That you are, my love," her mother said, running a fond hand down the girl's tentacle. Then she distributed the burgers to her children, shared out the drinks, and dumped all of the fries out on the tray together, next to several small containers of hot sauce. Dorothy's mouth and eyes began watering at the same time.

"Want some?" the oldest boy teased her, wiggling a fry.

97

"Gurk!" his mother scolded. "You know that the poor Humans can't eat their own food."

"But it's not our food," Dorothy protested. "It's your food, but rebranded."

"I never had anything like this growing up," the Drazen woman responded. "It's so delicious that I would have remembered."

"What I meant is that we can eat burgers and fries when they're made from our food rather than your food. We invented them, after all."

"What's the Human saying?" chorused the children, who obviously lacked implants.

"She feels bad about not being able to eat their food, just like in the song I translated for you," the mother said.

"Hrumph," Dorothy muttered, not wanting to get into an argument.

"That reminds me," the mother continued, pausing to rummage through her belt pouch and bringing out a coin. "Go put that in the poor Human's tip jar, Gurk. I saw in a documentary that they need to send money home for their relatives who aren't fortunate enough to find a job working for an advanced species."

Nine

"You've been disqualified," the Vergallian clerk declared, pushing the registration chit back at Samuel. "Somebody filed a complaint."

"This is the first I'm hearing about it," the ambassador's son replied in flawless Vergallian. "According to the regulations of the Regional Junior Ballroom Championships, no contestants shall be disqualified without a hearing before a full board meeting of the regents."

"As you're familiar with the regulations, I'm sure you're aware that there's an exception if the complaint is accompanied by incontrovertible evidence that a contestant is over the age limit. You're welcome to compete in the Regional Open Ballroom Championships—for adults."

"But he won't be seventeen for three more months," Vivian protested.

"You're talking about Human years. The rules committee is required to prorate the ages of aliens according to their life spans, and the multiplier for your species is…" the clerk paused, and his left eye darted back and forth as he scanned through a document on his heads-up display, "three, which I think is a generous understatement."

"Do I look forty-eight years old to you?" Samuel demanded.

"Rules are rules," the clerk replied. "Your entry fee has already been refunded to your programmable cred. Next?"

"Don't give him the satisfaction of getting mad," Vivian whispered. "We can't force our way into a dance competition if they don't want us."

"I'm only angry on your account," he said, giving Vivian his arm in proper Vergallian style and leading her back towards where their families were waiting. "I know how much you wanted to win, and I think we would have had a chance this year, even though we haven't been practicing as much lately."

The girl came to a halt, forcing Samuel to stop as well. "I only kept competing because I thought you wanted to. I love to dance, but I'd rather be studying tango with Aunt Chastity and Chance. The only thing I like about Vergallian ballroom style is that the heels are so high I can look at you without straining my neck."

The two teens stared at each other for a moment and then burst out laughing. But their families were waiting just a few paces away, so they regained control much more quickly than would have been the case otherwise.

"What's so funny?" Jonah demanded of his twin. "Did they put you at the end of the list for the first round again?"

"We've been disqualified," Vivian replied, struggling to keep a straight face. "Samuel's too old. Our ages have been prorated for life span."

"What?" Kelly exploded. "I'm going to go have a word with those jerks, and if they don't want to play fair, Ambassador Abeva can find herself another first contact mission to join."

"Wait," her son protested, grabbing her arm. "Hold her, Dad. It's okay, Mom. Vivian and I were only competing to make each other happy. We've both had enough of it."

"Finally," Blythe said, hugging her daughter and giving her a kiss. "You don't know how sick of Vergallian music we all are. And I was beginning to worry we'd have to take you to the Farling for toe surgery if you kept on wearing those shoes."

"The shoes are the only part I like, Mom," the girl replied, drawing a supportive wink from Chastity.

"I'll miss getting everybody from both families together for a night out," Donna said. "You're all so busy now."

"We have plenty of picnics in Mac's Bones," Joe pointed out.

"She's right," Kelly said. "It's different to get together as a group and actually go somewhere."

"I heard that a bowling alley just opened up next to the Shuk where there used to be an archery range," Stanley suggested. "I'm kind of curious to see how the station spin affects the game."

"What's a bowling alley?" Jonah asked.

"It's easier to show than to explain," Stanley replied to his grandson. "How about it?"

"If we're ever going to go bowling, let's do it now while the shoes are still new," Joe said.

"What does that mean?" Chastity asked, bouncing on her heels to calm her fidgeting baby.

"You'll see when we get there," Stanley repeated, encouraging the group to move in the direction of the lift tubes. "I'm buying."

Everybody squeezed into a single lift tube capsule, where Joe and Stanley engaged in their usual argument over who would pick up the check, finally compromising on the former paying for refreshments and the latter for the lanes. At the same time, Kelly attempted to explain bowling to everybody who hadn't grown up on Earth, but her own memories of the sport were confused, and she found that the main thing that stuck with her was the noise.

The counterman looked up when the group entered the bowling alley and did a double-take. "What do you know? You'll be my first human customers since I left Earth. I'm John Cote, and I want to welcome you to Union Station Candlepins."

Stanley took the opportunity to introduce the whole crew before asking, "How long have you been open here?"

"Just three days," John replied. "I didn't do any pre-publicity on the human deck because I wanted a chance to get the word out with the aliens first. How did you hear about us?"

"Come to think of it, I must have seen something in the correspondence stream for Eccentric Enterprises. I'm one of the outside auditors."

"I guess a bowling alley on a space station qualifies as eccentric," Kelly commented.

"Eccentric Enterprises," Blythe said, stressing the name. "Have you forgotten already?"

"Wait. Is that the franchising outfit you set up for the President?"

"He didn't want to call it 'EarthCent Enterprises' because everybody would have confused it with the diplomatic arm. It's all run from Earth, but we're providing financing and business intelligence."

"Sounds like I owe you thanks for my startup loan," John said. "After thirty years of doing business on Earth, I couldn't believe how fast everything happened after I made my proposal to Eccentric."

"Why did you want to get the word out to aliens before advertising to humans?" Kelly asked.

"Well, that's a long story, but I'll make it short. I inherited an old candlepin alley from my folks, and I just couldn't bring myself to shut it down, even though business got worse and worse every year. I stopped maintaining half of the lanes, turned off the lights on that side of the building to save money, even cannibalized the unused pin setting machines to keep the active lanes going. But I would have given up a couple of years ago if not for the Dollnicks."

"The Dollnicks bowl?"

"No, well, some of them, but it's not their main interest. Turns out there's a game they play back home that has to do with setting up pins. A group of Dolly managers from the radioactive materials recycling plant came in one night and asked if I would let them have a go at it, sort of a friendly competition. I turned off the pin setters and let them set up for the local league, and you never saw such fast frames in your life. Everybody had a great time, which is where I got the idea to pitch Eccentric."

"To improve Earth's visibility with aliens through bowling?" Chastity asked, sensing a human interest story for the Galactic Free Press.

"This is just a pop-up alley, a proof of concept before we roll the franchise out to alien worlds, if you'll pardon the pun."

"I understand pop-up retail shops to test market ideas, but how do you open a temporary bowling alley?" Kelly asked.

"Go ahead, kids," the owner addressed the teens, whose attention was focused on the active bowlers. "You're on lanes fifteen and sixteen. I wish I could give you four lanes, but the rest are all reserved. And don't forget to stick your feet in the Drazen foot wrappers before you start. Do the same before you leave or you'll have to cut them off at home." Then he turned back to Kelly and continued his story. "I couldn't justify renting enough space on a Stryx station for a bowling alley because I'd have to charge a hundred creds an hour for a lane. By doing it in temporary space, the station manager cut me a serious discount."

"I meant installing the lanes and the equipment."

"There is no equipment, that's the whole point. The Dollys pay to set up the pins and roll the balls back, though a posse of Drazens came in here last night and challenged them for the positions. But when it comes to pin setting, four arms beats two arms and a tentacle every day of the week."

"Can I invite Mikey?" Fenna asked her mother.

"That's a good idea," Aisha said. "Are you going to have Libby ping his house, or should I try?"

"I'll ask Libby," the girl replied, and turning away so she wouldn't bother the grown-ups, called for the station librarian's attention without a trace of self-consciousness.

"So how did you get the lanes in so quickly?" Joe asked. "I've never seen as much wood in one place on the station."

"It's not real wood," John admitted. "The Frunge would have made a fuss, and there's no point starting out in business setting anybody's hair vines on end. It's a quick-drying cement that the Drazens use for leveling their version of shuffleboard courts, but it's printed to look like wood, and according to the supplier, the finish will hold up for decades as long as everybody uses the foot wrappers. The lanes are in line with the station's spin, so physics doesn't cause problems, and you can barely notice the curvature over sixty feet."

"You seem to know a lot about alien cultures for some-body who lived on Earth until recently," the ambassador observed.

"I mentioned that business was slow, but I still had to be there twelve hours a day, so I might have spent too much time watching Grenouthian documentaries," John allowed. "Anyway, the foot wrappers are calibrated for the right coefficient of friction, and they save the whole hassle of having to stock and sanitize rental shoes, not to mention carrying all of the sizes for aliens."

"Would you like to do an interview for the Galactic Free Press?" Chastity asked. "I could see it as a weekend feature."

"Let me think about it," the owner replied. "I wouldn't want to get overrun by humans to the point that the aliens stop coming. The whole point of opening on the station is to tweak the business model."

"How about I send a reporter to do the interview, but I promise to sit on the story until you're ready. I'm the publisher."

John glanced away at a group of rambunctious Grenouthians who had just entered the bowling alley and were hopping towards them. "I'll tell you what. I'll come over to your lanes to talk when I finish up here, but I've got to take care of these bunnies first. They reserved a lane each and they bowl continuously for hours on end. I think they're trying to wear out the Dollnicks."

"Nice meeting you," Joe said for everybody, and they headed over to their designated lanes. The kids already had their feet wrapped and were trying to figure out what to do next by watching the other bowlers, all of whom seemed to be playing different games.

"Everybody slide in," Blythe ordered. "It's going to be a tight squeeze."

"I'm going to go get some refreshments, and there's seating behind the benches for the people who aren't bowling." Joe said. "Come and carry, Stan?"

"I'll help," Clive volunteered. "Pop's probably the only one who knows the rules."

"Do you know the rules, Grandpa?" Vivian asked.

"Let me get my feet wrapped," Stanley said. "I don't want to scratch up the lanes." He inserted first one foot and then the other into the Drazen foot wrapper. There was a hissing sound as something was sprayed right over the shoe, followed by an intense blue light that cured the liquid, and each foot came out sheathed in a flexible white substance.

"Where are your shoes?" Blythe asked her daughter, who was suddenly a half a head shorter than she had been a few minutes earlier.

"I don't care how good the Drazen technology is, I'm not letting it spray stuff on my dancing shoes," Vivian replied.

"You had your bare feet wrapped?"

"I've got hose on, and besides, I checked with Libby and it's perfectly safe. Drazens who live on swampy worlds wrap their bare legs all the way to the hip instead of wearing shoes and pants."

"All right, kids," Stanley said, rushing through a few perfunctory stretches and picking up a ball. "There aren't any finger holes in these, unlike the bigger balls used in Ten-pin bowling, so just hold on the best you can and roll the ball down the middle of the lane until you get the hang of it. Watch me."

Stanley took three steps, terminated in a graceful glide, and launched the first ball down the lane. It hooked to the right and fell into the gutter.

"Nice bid," snorted a young Horten in the next lane. He winked at his three friends, who all contributed to a sarcastic chorus.

"Are you going to leave them like that?"

"You must be in a league."

"I've never seen it done like that before."

"Just ignore them, Dad," Blythe said. "You probably haven't played in forty years."

"Thanks for reminding me," Stanley grumbled, grabbing a second ball. This time his luck was a little better, and the ball knocked down six pins, leaving a set that looked like a gap-toothed smile. "Now, watch me as I pick up the spare." The third ball described a graceful curve towards the lead pin on the left side, then slipped through the gap without touching wood.

As Stanley returned to his seat and Jonah stood up to take his place, Donna exclaimed, "Hey, the pins are back up again already. I forgot to watch for the Dollnick."

"You take turns with Grandpa, and Samuel and I will play against you in the other lane," Vivian told her brother.

"All right," Jonah said, taking a ball from the return. He stared down the Horten kids before striding forward and releasing it like he'd been bowling all of his life. The ball hooked right into the front of the formation, pins flew, and a moment later, there were only two left standing, one at each corner. The combined McAllister and Doogal clans cheered.

"Aim for the pin that's lying down out front," Vivian suggested. "It might fly into the one on the right, and then the ball will go left."

107

"Don't get greedy," Stanley advised his grandson. "Just try picking them off one at a time. You get three balls a frame in candlepin."

"Why are you helping him?" Samuel complained to Vivian, having barely clipped one pin off the corner with his own first roll.

Jonah took another ball, executed a graceful slide, and released. Just before his ball reached its target, the pin disappeared in a blur, then rematerialized after the ball passed harmlessly through the space it had occupied.

"What was that?" Kelly cried. "Is the whole thing a hologram?"

"Sorry," the owner said, coming up behind the curved couch seat, which was covered with an imitation leather fabric. "The Dollnicks can't help themselves sometimes. Fast, aren't they?"

"You mean a Dolly grabbed the pin right before the ball hit and then put it back?" Stanley asked.

"Yeah. The way they play at home involves another player swinging a long bat at the pins, but they seem to think that this is actually better." The manager put two fingers in his mouth and gave a piercing whistle that rose and fell like a complex birdsong. "There. I told them to lay off on the early pin grabs until you get warmed up."

"You speak Dollnick?" Kelly asked in astonishment. "I didn't know that was possible."

"Just enough to get by on this type of stuff," John said modestly. "When I needed a break from Grenouthian documentaries back on Earth, I started watching lots of alien sports, especially paddle-cup-mitt-ball. You pick up some of the lingo after a while if you pay attention to the subtitles, but the Dollnick children make fun of my accent."

Joe and Clive returned with a variety of drinks in plastic cups and a large assortment of snack food, and everybody ate while watching the team of Stanley and Jonah eke out a win against Samuel and Vivian. The deciding factor was that the Dollnick setting pins in lane sixteen kept subtly varying the spacing to make it harder to knock them all down.

Shaina arrived with her son and Spinner, and everybody agreed to let Fenna, Mike, and the little Stryx go next. Paul joined in to make the teams even, and the aliens in adjacent lanes on both sides stopped to watch when the little robot took a ball in his pincer and floated up to the line. Then he spun around a few times for momentum and released the ball, which shot down the lane like it had been flung from a slingshot. The pins scattered with a crash, and Fenna and Mike cheered.

"Strike!" Stanley shouted triumphantly in the direction of the Hortens.

"How did you do that?" Mike asked his friend.

"It's just math," Spinner said modestly. "I could teach you, if you could float and spin and do vector calculus, I mean."

"I'm not spinning," Fenna said, taking her turn at the line and rolling the ball with both hands from between her legs. It made its way lazily down the center of the lane, impacting the pins with barely enough velocity to knock a few over.

Blythe nudged her husband and indicated the owner of the bowling alley, at the same time making an "O" shape with her thumb and forefinger, holding it up near her chest like a badge.

"Right," Clive said, standing up and accompanying John back towards the register. "So, you're planning on opening up on alien worlds in the near future?"

"We're going to focus on Dollnick planets for the time being, since they're the most enthusiastic and we can get them to play at both ends. Bowling would be a natural fit for Dollnick open worlds with humans, but Eccentric Enterprises is more interested in extending human visibility to alien homeworlds."

"Did you know that there's a program that may cover the cost of certain employees deployed to alien worlds in return for a flexible work schedule?"

"You mean EarthCent Intelligence?"

"Somebody from Eccentric spilled the beans?"

"No, but one of the Dollnicks who approached me about a franchise brought it up as a way to reduce labor costs. He said it's pretty much assumed that all alien businesses employ spies. It's lucky that I'm meeting you because there's a special form he said I'll need to get somebody from EarthCent Intelligence to fill out for each agent he employs in his bowling alley."

Ten

"I'm glad you decided to come along, Dring," Kelly told the Maker. "I've never been so nervous. I feel like some of the other ambassadors are just waiting for me to make a mistake so they can step in and save the day."

"Don't forget that Stryx Wylx is ultimately responsible for the success or failure of the mission," Dring reminded her. "The rest of us are only here to put a friendly face on the tunnel network."

"That's why I'm dressing casual. Dorothy would go crazy if she saw me, but if I were a member of another species meeting aliens for the first time, I'd feel more comfortable if they didn't all look like they were dressed for a funeral."

"An interesting outlook. I believe we should start for the reception hall if we want to be early."

"Early is on time," Kelly replied reflexively.

The science ship was constructed like a miniature version of Union Station, and Stryx Wylx was maintaining a rotational rate that brought their weight in the guest residential area to something like ninety percent of Earth normal. The trip to the Alt homeworld had taken four days, just enough time to keep the biologicals from feeling the side effects of jumping long distances too quickly.

"Dring. Kelly," Bork greeted them in the corridor. He was resplendent in some type of military uniform that the EarthCent ambassador had never seen him wear. "An exciting moment awaits us."

"I'm sure it will be of great historical interest," Dring concurred. "I have never attended an Opening negotiation for obvious reasons."

"Ambassadors. Maker," Czeros said, emerging from his cabin clad in a stunning metallic suit that flowed like water. "I can't remember ever being this excited about a meeting. In fact, I can't remember ever being excited by any meeting before this one."

"You don't feel overdressed?" Kelly hinted to her colleagues.

"My wife insisted," Bork said. "She expects the press to publish images of the meeting and she wanted me to look my best."

"And I received an intelligence report just before we left Union Station," Czeros told the EarthCent ambassador. "I would have let you know, but I assumed your daughter would take advantage of the opportunity to wrap you in designer fashions."

"She's away, and what do you mean about an intelligence report? You spied on how the other ambassadors would be dressed?"

"A strategic wardrobe assessment," Czeros explained. "A good offense is the best defense."

"Why does the universe have to be so weird?" Kelly muttered to Dring as they rounded the corridor to the appointed meeting place.

A small knot of Union Station ambassadors stood outside the reception hall, looking like characters from an opera. Half of them wore dress military uniforms with elaborate hats, several others were dressed like Czeros, in state-of-the-art fabrics of native manufacture. Even the Grenouthian ambassador, who at most wore a sash on fancy occasions, was draped in a sort of cloak that was studded with jewels and heavily embroidered with thread made from precious metals.

"Interesting choice of wardrobe," the Vergallian ambassador addressed Kelly. "If you're wearing that because the Stryx lost your luggage, I believe I have a bathrobe that would fit you while providing a significant upgrade."

"My only goal is to put the Alts at ease," Kelly retorted with a confidence she didn't entirely feel. "Why are you all standing in the corridor?"

"Jeeves said that the doors will be unlocked on time," Ambassador Crute responded. "The Alts have already arrived and they are negotiating directly with the Stryx before meeting the rest of us."

"I thought we were supposed to be here to break the whole AI thing to them gently," Kelly murmured to Dring, who shrugged his scaly shoulders. She kept an eye on her ornamental wristwatch while the other ambassadors all fidgeted with their uniforms and fancy clothes, and finally the doors slid open. Jeeves floated out, extending his pincer to prevent them from surging into the room, and the doors closed again behind him.

"It's all set," the young Stryx said. "Before you go in, a few words of advice. First, it's clear that family is an indivisible unit in Alt society, so don't be surprised that the members of their delegation are accompanied by spouses, children, and even a few grandparents. Second, they are somewhat more expressive than the typical tunnel network species, to the point where several of them kissed me." Here Jeeves spun around slowly, displaying a series of smudges along his casing.

"They're going to touch our clothes?" Abeva asked in horror.

"If you hurry and change into your bathrobe, I'll make an excuse for you," Kelly offered facetiously.

"And if you'll permit me to finish," Jeeves continued, floating between the two ambassadors. "The Alts were expecting us. It turns out they already know quite a bit about the tunnel network through passive monitoring of some of your public broadcasts. They couldn't access the Stryxnet, of course, but they've been very innovative about intercepting radio frequency signals, especially those from Earth. The Alts delayed development of faster-than-light drive much longer than one would expect for a species of their technological prowess because they felt that the risks outweighed the rewards."

"Ah," Dring commented softly, apparently deriving some meaning from this last statement that wasn't immediately clear to Kelly.

"I've updated all of your implants, and I've provided compatible equivalency tables for the earpiece translation technology developed by the Alts, so you should be able to communicate reasonably well." The door to the reception hall slid open, and Jeeves announced, "Ladies and Gentlemen of the Alts. I present to you the tunnel network ambassadors who breathe a similar mix of gasses."

A group of little children charged the ambassadors and began hugging their legs and waists. One boy got a grip on Bork's tentacle and tried to pull himself up the Drazen's back, and the ambassador obligingly extended that appendage to its full length, so the child could clamber up onto his shoulder. Two more children grabbed Crute's lower set of arms and began swinging on them, while a teenage boy was frozen in place, ogling Abeva with his mouth open.

114

"My youngest," an Alt woman said, passing her baby to Srythlan, who cradled the infant cautiously. The Grenouthian ambassador picked up a little girl who was tugging on his cloak and deposited her feet-first into his belly pouch, where she peered out like a baby kangaroo.

"Let us eat together," declared a handsome Alt man, who could have passed as Vergallian. He indicated the large table surrounded by chairs, each place setting a cornucopia overflowing with fruits. "The Stryx have assured us that our native bounty may be safely consumed by all of you."

"I'm Ambassador McAllister," Kelly introduced herself to the man who she took to be the Alt leader. "The Stryx appointed me head of the biological contingent of this mission because you jumped into our system."

"I am honored to…" the man began to reply, but at that moment the Alt infant who was being pressed into Kelly's arms began to scream at the top of his lungs. All of the conversations in the room came to an instant halt, and the mother snatched her baby back from the ambassador. He stopped screaming immediately, but refused to look in Kelly's direction.

"I don't know what's come over him," the woman said to the Alt leader. "I'm so embarrassed, Madame Ambassador."

"What are your names?" Kelly asked.

"Methan," the leader replied. "My wife, Rinla, and you just met our youngest son, Methanon. The others are busy climbing on your colleagues."

"Does 'Methanon' mean 'Son of Methan?'"

The Alt couple exchanged a puzzled look before Rinla answered, "No. It's a type of flower."

"Does this one belong to you?" Bork asked, approaching them with the boy still sitting on his shoulder. The child was holding onto the Drazen's ears for balance, and the ambassador kept his tentacle wrapped around the boy's waist to keep him steady.

"Antha!" his mother admonished her child with a smile. "Don't pull on the nice alien's ears. Say 'Hello' to Ambassador McAllister. Doesn't she look like your Aunt Felda?"

"Don't want to," the boy replied, letting go of Bork's ears, but folding his arms over the alien's tentacle to keep it in place. "She's scary."

"Scary?" Kelly and the adult Alts asked simultaneously.

"Like a big cat," the boy said, half daring the EarthCent ambassador to contradict him.

"Maybe it's my green eyes," Kelly suggested.

"Felda has green eyes," Methan replied. "They're quite common in our people. Red hair as well."

"You and Ambassador McAllister look to me like you could be from the same planet, and I don't mean that as an 'all aliens look alike' joke," Bork commented. He took a seat at the table and extended his tentacle to deposit the boy in the chair next to him. "So who's your favorite tunnel network species?" he prompted.

"Drazens!" the boy shouted happily.

Crute took a seat on the other side of the table, where the two children who had been swinging on his lower arms scrambled into his lap. He kept them both amused by simultaneously peeling two pieces of fruit, using the upper arm from one side with the lower of the other on each piece, just to show off. The remaining ambassadors found places, interspersed between Alt representatives or their family members, but when Kelly tried to sit next to a little girl, the child disappeared under the table. Methan took

116

the seat on one side of the EarthCent ambassador and Dring waddled up to the table on the other side, remaining standing, as was his fashion.

"I don't understand," Kelly said. "I have children of my own, and I've always gotten along well with the little ones of the other species."

Methan shrugged. "Our children are highly empathic so they probably took their cue from the baby." He leaned forward a bit and smiled at the Maker. "Hello. Please help yourself to some fruit."

"Thank you," Dring replied, picking something that looked like a stalk of raw rhubarb out of the woven cornucopia and giving it an experimental chew. "Excellent."

"All of you seem very comfortable meeting aliens for the first time," Kelly couldn't help remarking to Methan. "Have you had other visitors before us?"

"We've been aware of the other species for some time. We also suspected that our space was somehow hidden from the outside, which is why when we perfected our jump drive, we popped into your system for just a moment to take a look back and confirm the fact. It's been clear to us for tens of generations that we were moved to our current home by some benevolent species. Our sociologists claim that the knowledge has had a strong influence on our culture."

"How did you know that you'd been moved?"

"The geology of our world makes no sense," Methan elaborated. "The fossil record stretches back thirty thousand years or so, and before that, nothing. As near as we can tell, our planet was a lifeless ball of rock until somebody prepared it for our arrival and then transported our ancestors and their ecosystem here to inhabit it. We now know that that somebody was Stryx Wylx, though she hasn't elaborated on her reasons."

"Have you ever heard of your Stryx doing anything similar, Dring?" Kelly asked.

The Maker paused his enthusiastic mastication long enough to reply, "Yes, on rare occasions."

"Excuse me," Methan addressed Kelly. "Did you imply that the Stryx belong in some way to our reptilian friend?"

"Dring? He's a Maker. They're pretty much immortal, and his people created the Stryx nearly a hundred million years ago when it looked like a race of killer AI was going to destroy all life in the galaxy. The Makers intended the Stryx to run away and survive, but instead they came back and won the war, saving the biologicals."

"And now they've taken on the role of the galaxy's nannies, approaching species who develop faster-than-light drive and helping them integrate into a peaceful society?"

Kelly hastily swallowed a mouthful of delicious fruit that reminded her of peach before replying. "It's more complicated than that. The Stryx don't recruit species to the tunnel network if there's already an empire or some other form of government in the region, and a good chunk of the galaxy belongs to an ancient race of vacuum-dwelling dragons who aren't crazy about outsiders. The Stryx don't always fill us in on the details."

"Was your system hidden from the rest of the galaxy before you developed faster-than-light-drive?" Methan asked.

Kelly took her time finishing the peach while formulating her answer. "We were invited to join the tunnel network as probationary members before our technology advanced that far. It's a sort of an outreach program the Stryx sometimes extend…"

"To species who are on the verge of destroying them-selves or being invaded," Abeva interrupted from the other side of the table. "These purple fruits are scrumptious, even better than Earth lemons."

"How did you know that you weren't the survivors of a colony ship?" Kelly asked Methan. "Your people might have lost their original technology in a disaster and then slowly reinvented it all."

"Some of our fiction writers did explore those themes, but the evidence pointed to a history of continuous devel-opment starting from a primitive level," Methan replied. "I could show you images of our early cave art, which is very well preserved, and someday the Stryx might clear you to visit our world, though I was cautioned not to extend an invitation at this point."

"So they're still protecting you from pushy aliens," Kelly said with a smile.

The Alt leader coughed and averted his face for a mo-ment. "Actually, Stryx Wylx didn't say anything about the other aliens."

"It's just humans who are banned?"

"Uh, some humans," the Alt qualified.

"Just me?"

"No, no," Methan protested. "Stryx Wylx also cau-tioned us against inviting two young correspondents who recently left your homeworld."

"I'm glad to see everybody getting along so well," Jeeves said, floating up behind the ambassador. The room fell silent as everybody waited to see what the Stryx had to say. "I just popped out for a look at your ship, Methan, and while it's likely capable of reaching Union Station and returning, Stryx Wylx and I will feel much better if you accept our hospitality for this trip."

"You've already agreed to come visit?" Kelly asked the Alt leader.

"We could hardly turn down such an invitation, especially as it originates with our benefactor," Methan replied. "I would have preferred to make the voyage in our own ship for the sake of gathering technical data, but I bow to your superior knowledge," he concluded, literally bowing his head in the direction of Jeeves.

Immediately, every one of the ambassadors present began pitching the nearest Alt adult on a visit to their respective embassies back on Union Station. Crute managed to keep up a game of cat's cradle with each of the children on his lap while extending offers of hospitality to both sides, his head snapping back and forth like that of an observer at a tennis match. Kelly overheard Bork appointing his young Alt friend as an honorary Drazen ambassador and sending him off on a mission to recruit others of his kind to the cause, while Czeros launched into a demonstration of how the metallic fabric of his outfit could instantly conform to and hold any shape.

"So, everything is already settled about your joining the tunnel network," the EarthCent ambassador surmised.

"That decision will be taken by my people at some point in the future," Methan replied. "My mandate extends to visiting a Stryx station on an inspection tour, but I'll only have one voice when the time comes to discuss the matter. My colleagues and I were chosen for this task because we crewed the jump ship to your system and were still onboard when the Stryx invitation was received. While we have established bases on the moons of several of the planets orbiting our sun, all of the individuals living on those are already engaged in important tasks of their own. Likewise, our launch capacity is scheduled well in advance, and while we could have rushed another team into orbit, the crew of the 'Long Jump' has already been through first contact training."

"We named our first faster-than-light ship the 'Long Jump' as well," Bork contributed.

"Everybody does," Abeva chipped in from across the table. "Everybody who develops faster-than-light drive, I mean."

"So let me make sure I have this straight," Kelly said. "Here you are, aware that there's other sentient life in the galaxy, some of it far more technologically advanced than your own civilization, and you develop a faster-than-light drive. You delay using it because you're not that sure you want to meet the rest of us, and when you do take the first jump, your primary mission is to look back at your home system to confirm that it's invisible from the outside."

"That's right," the Alt confirmed.

"Then you're contacted by Stryx Wylx, who informs you that she is responsible for moving you to your world, and that there's a network of tunnels interconnecting tens of thousands of other worlds that you're invited to join. Your people decide to welcome an outreach mission, which arrives within weeks, and now your crew and families agree to visit Union Station in return."

"Yes, that's it."

"When the Stryx contacted my own world, there were riots in the streets. Nobody wanted to accept the fact that sentient machines existed, not to mention that they were so much smarter than us. My parents were just children at the time, but they didn't go to school for nearly a year because governments were collapsing and nobody could figure out how to pay the teachers. But your people welcome both the Stryx and alien ambassadors with open arms and agree

121

to visit a space station halfway across the galaxy as if you were spending a weekend with friends!"

"I hope you do think of us as friends," Methan said with a smile.

"And it's not halfway across the galaxy," Jeeves put in. "More like a twentieth. Speaking of which, I think we've kept the press and your trade reps waiting in the corridor long enough."

The door to the room slid open, allowing in the volunteers from Pub Haggis, two Children's News Network reporters in their mid-teens, Chastity, and a Galactic Free Press photographer loaded down with 3D imaging equipment. The Alt children held back from rushing to greet the influx of humans, and Kelly would have sworn she saw one or two of them actually hiding behind alien ambassadors.

"Official image," Chastity announced. "Everybody up, now. I think four lines arranged by height with the tallest in the center would be best. Morty?"

"It's going to take me a few minutes to set all this junk up," the cameraman told her.

"It's all right," Jeeves said, floating out to greet them, "Wylx can take much nicer images in any case."

"Why are we even here?" Kelly mouthed at Chastity, as everybody lined up for the 3D image. Fortunately, the first two lines were made up entirely of young Alts, so the smallest children who were obviously uncomfortable around humans had an adolescent Alt as a buffer behind them.

Eleven

"He's going to be mad when he wakes up," Kevin warned Dorothy.

"But it will help keep his claws from chipping, and black is a masculine color."

"He looks like a goth Cayl hound, and Beowulf is going to laugh at him. Besides, that chipping is part of the process that keeps his nails from getting so long that they need to be clipped. I still get the shivers when I think about taking care of Borgia's claws when I was a kid and cutting one too close. She yelped and started bleeding—the look she gave me—it was like I betrayed her to a cat. It was heartbreaking."

"You're such a softie. If Alex's nails need clipping, I'll do it," Dorothy said, putting away the little bottle of protective lacquer. "I just hope it has time to dry before we get to the elevator."

"That won't be a problem because I'm not waking him. The Frunge don't allow alien dog breeds on their worlds. Their own dogs are too territorial, which is why you don't see any of them on mixed species stations."

"Oh, that explains why Flazint makes such a fuss over our dogs. I never thought to ask."

"I'm hoping that the special visa from your mother's friend will speed things up, so we can visit Flazint's cousin, deliver the gifts, and then get a week's worth of trading in

123

at the elevator hub. I've been to Frunge worlds before and there are merchants who specialize in bringing trade goods up to the elevator hub by the container load."

"But what do we have that they'll want?"

"You never know with aliens, that's the fun part. There's no market at a fully developed world for the kinds of commodities and species-specific goods that go well at small space stations or on the frontier, but if I lay out enough odds and ends, it usually turns out that something is trending. One time at a Frunge elevator hub, I traded a box of Verlock memory-metal drinking cups that cost me less than fifty creds for a decorative suit of armor that I later disposed of for ten times that. And after we knuckled on the deal, the Frunge merchant told me that each one of those cups was worth a whole suit of armor on the surface at the moment. That's the best kind of trade, where you both win."

"So why wouldn't they ship all of their suits of armor to wherever you sold yours and make a killing?"

"Because markets aren't static, it's all about timing. And I didn't actually get five hundred creds cash for that suit of armor. A few weeks later, I took four princely measures of Dollnick tubers in trade, which practically filled the hold of my old ship."

"What did you want with a bunch of potatoes we can't eat?"

"I was heading for Prince Kluge's space docks to barter for spare parts that a human colony on a Dollnick open world needed, and fresh tubers always go like hotcakes to Dollys living in space."

"How did you know that the colonists needed spare parts, or that they wouldn't already have them by the time you got there?"

"It was in the trader supplement of the Galactic Free Press," Kevin explained. "Full subscribers can put a lock on orders they intend to fill within the time limit."

"But what if somebody just locked a bunch of orders to try to get rich and then didn't fill them?"

"You can only lock one open requisition at a time, and if you don't fulfill it, you lose your locking privilege for ten cycles. Everybody is really careful about that."

"So the colonists paid you five hundred in cash?"

"No, they paid me in T-shirts, which I took to..."

"So how do you know that the suit of armor was worth five hundred creds if you just kept recycling it into more stuff?" the girl interrupted.

"It's all in the logs. You have to keep good books as a trader."

"Why?" Dorothy cried. "It's your ship, your goods, nobody is charging you any taxes. What difference does it make as long as you come out ahead?"

"How would I know I was coming out ahead if I didn't keep records? Besides, I have to supply the Stryx with a manifest every time we use a tunnel if I want to get the profit sharing discount rather than paying the regular toll."

"I thought that was only for ships carrying Earth exports!"

"They give small traders plenty of wiggle room, and believe me, there are times the Stryx come out ahead on the deal. Once when I was cash rich, I gambled on a shipping container of athletic sleeves at an auction. They were incredibly cheap, and I thought they would trade well, since most species strain a muscle now and then and the sleeves were made of good stretchy stuff. A cycle later, I stopped at a Drazen station for fuel, and it turned out

125

that the weather control satellites for the nearby colony were saturated and the place was in a deep freeze. A local seamstress saw the sleeves and snapped them all up to stitch together as tentacle warmers. She paid cash, and I tripled my money just like that."

"So you had to give a percentage to the Stryx the next time you used a tunnel?"

"They just skimmed their cut off my programmable cred when we did the transaction. Hey, we're here already."

The traffic control alert began to flash and ding, and Kevin hit the manual override switch to hand over control of the ship. As soon as they were docked, Dorothy was at the hatch with her daypack, ready to exit.

"This is exciting," she said. "Flazint told me that the sun here is red."

"You packed a sunhat and plenty of protective cream, right? The Frunge like worlds that will give humans wicked sunburns in nothing flat."

"I've got everything I need for a three-day outing right here. It looks like you're bringing enough for a month. I thought you said no trading on the surface."

"Did you want to carry some of Flazint's gifts?"

"Oh, I forgot." The safety interlock released and the hatch popped open. "Magnetic cleats on. Let's go. Let me do the talking in customs this time."

Kevin shouldered his pack and followed Dorothy into the docking arm. A metal conveyer belt zipped them along to a large open space which proved to be the customs hall. Fortunately, there was no queue, and Dorothy was soon presenting the special visa that Ambassador Czeros had happily provided for them.

"Theros, an old pal of mine," the female customs agent said.

"Czeros," Dorothy corrected her.

"Right, Czeros. Did he mention that he owed me, uh, fifty creds?"

"The ambassador told me that it was twenty," Dorothy replied, giving special stress to the job title. Then she put on a bright smile and offered the Frunge woman a handshake, during which she transferred a twenty cred coin that she had secreted between her middle and ring fingers in preparation. The customs agent pocketed it without looking, proving that she could tell currency denominations by feel.

"All right then. Are the two of you together?" the agent asked.

"Yes. I'm sure that the ambassador said he owed you twenty for the both of us."

"I don't see any rings or tattoos. Are you siblings?"

"Just friends."

"What's that supposed to mean? Do you think you can tip me to turn my head from immoral behavior?" the Frunge woman demanded indignantly.

"She didn't understand your question," Kevin interjected. "I have our companionship contract right here." He twisted out of his backpack and removed the stone slab, passing it to the customs agent.

The Frunge woman carefully read the tablet before handing it back and sniffing in disdain. "Pretty weak terms, but I've heard that Stryx stations are dens of iniquity. If you want to ruin your life, young lady, that's your business. Next."

"Where did you learn how to bribe a customs agent like that?" Kevin demanded as they headed for the elevator.

"The EarthCent Intelligence training camp has been my front yard for years. I'm not as into it as Samuel, but I guess I've been through most of the training once or twice, and it's starting to come back to me. How long is it going to take to reach the surface?"

"I haven't been here before, but the Frunge elevators run a variable grip system, so the cars really zip along until we hit the atmosphere. Probably less than a day. It's all bunk seating in any case, so we can catch up on our sleep."

Twenty hours later the couple emerged into the bright red sunlight, stepping carefully as they allowed their bodies to acclimate to the gravity. A Frunge woman with a towering trellis construction on her head and two shrubs in tow waved excitedly at them from behind the chain separating the waiting area from the exit. Even without the enthusiastic greeting, Dorothy would have recognized the family from the SBJ Fashions travel cloaks all three sported.

"Barzee," Dorothy greeted the young mother. "You look just like your holo images."

The Frunge woman looked puzzled for a moment, then irritated, and she pulled out a tab and began swiping through menus.

"Bad language?" Kevin guessed.

"You speak Frunge!" Barzee said in surprise. "Yes, I bought a Humanese upgrade at the implant kiosk but it's not working."

"I only a small words speaking," Kevin replied, causing the children to burst out laughing, and then to cover their mouths. "Trader words."

"But the two of you understand me perfectly through your station implants, right? Good. Let's stop at the kiosk and I'll get my money back. I should have just bought the upgrade from the local travel agency, but I thought I'd save a few coins."

Barzee led them to a kiosk in the lobby of the elevator terminal where she immediately demanded a refund. The clerk pulled up the recent transaction from memory and shook his head, making a hand movement that cloned his holo display so the customers could see the same thing he was looking at.

"Humanese. I gave you the most advanced version, just like you asked."

"These are Humans and I can't understand a word that they're saying," Barzee complained.

"Hang on a sec," Kevin said, and both of the aliens paused to look at him without understanding his words. "Wrong Humanese," he explained in Frunge. "We different tongues speaking. You sell her Chinese, wanting English. This one," he concluded, pointing at the English text in the holographic list.

The clerk scratched his head and shrugged. "Apparently they speak all these different languages even though they're the same species," he told Barzee. "I thought these others were just all vocabulary-limited versions of the expensive one. Weird, huh?"

"Does that mean I'll get something back?" Barzee asked.

"Yeah, it's like thirty percent cheaper, but I have to outload the original one first." He pointed a device that looked like a small microwave dish at the Frunge woman's head. "Ready?"

"Learning mode enabled," Barzee responded.

"Done," he said almost instantly. The clerk swiped a hand above the register and the drawer popped open.

Then he extracted a few coins and slid them over the counter, where they were appropriated by the children.

"Can you hear me now?" Dorothy asked.

"I can understand you now," Flazint's cousin replied. "I could hear you before but it sounded like desert cats fighting. Welcome to our world. Let's grab the maglev and get out of the docks area. It's all wholesale import/export around here."

Dorothy walked next to Barzee, answering her questions about Flazint's courting life and SBJ Fashions, while Kevin found himself accompanying the two children, who kept on looking up at him and giggling. Talking to them with his limited trader Frunge only brought on temporary hysterics, so he settled for pointing at things and looking puzzled. The children quickly caught on, providing fanciful names for the objects.

The Frunge woman waved a pass as they entered the maglev station, and they took their seats on the waiting train. By the time it reached the mixed residential and retail complex where Barzee's family lived, the children were kneeling on the bench to either side of Kevin and pretending to find insects in his hair, which they offered him as snacks.

"I think they have me confused with a Dollnick," Kevin said. "Humans don't eat insects."

"You don't?" Barzee's face fell. "Well, let's just drop off your things and we'll go out for a bite to eat. You must be hungry after the elevator trip."

"I brought along extra ship's rations, just in case," Kevin said, thumping the pack at his feet. "We don't want to drag you all over the place looking for synthesizers."

"We aren't *that* far out of the galactic mainstream. There's even a store in this district that sells wine and cheese from your Earth, though it always seemed like an odd combination to me. My husband buys wine there, and he brought home a bag of chocolate-covered insects that were supposedly exported from your world. I thought you'd make a meal of them, but I guess the salesman was having him on," the Frunge woman concluded as the maglev came to a silent halt.

After a brief walk through a park area that consisted mainly of metal and stone sculptures, they were halted at the entrance of Barzee's complex by a gnarled old guard.

"What are these two?" he demanded.

"Humans," Barzee replied.

The doorman folded his arms across his chest and stayed right in front of them.

"You know what I mean."

"I'm sure they have a contract," the Frunge woman elucidated. "My cousin wouldn't associate with libertines."

"It's in the outside pouch of my pack," Kevin said, turning his back so Barzee could remove it.

The old doorman skimmed the terms and handed it back, limiting himself to the comment, "Kids these days."

"Why does everybody keep asking to see our contract?" Dorothy asked Barzee. "We only got it because your cousin insisted."

"Later," the Frunge woman said, indicating the children with a nod. "Little logs have big ears."

When they reached Barzee's apartment, she sent her children to water the grass, apparently a Frunge euphemism for trying the bathroom. While Kevin and Dorothy put their backpacks in the guestroom, the young mother rummaged through a storage closet and produced a shoulder bag with a transparent side.

"It's a contract carrier," she explained to Kevin. "It's better to have it with you in public since my people are convinced that aliens are all decadent. It's the fault of those Grenouthian documentaries."

"Do you watch them?" Dorothy asked.

"Everybody watches them," Barzee replied, though her hair vines changed shades in embarrassment. "I don't believe half of it, but it's important to see how other species live. Speaking of which, are there any special sights you wanted to see while you're here?"

"The petrified cities of ancestors," Kevin said immediately.

"And I promised Flazint that we would visit the closest metallurgical museum and buy lots of gift shop samples," Dorothy added.

"We have to take them to that place!" one of kids yelled from the bathroom, proving that little logs did have big ears. "You promised."

"And I'm hungry," the other child cried.

"It's on the way to the museum," Barzee called back to the shrubs. "My husband is planning to take you both to the petrified cities tomorrow," she continued, turning to Kevin. "He's long overdue to visit his ancestors anyway."

"Let's go already," the older child said, coming out of the bathroom and appropriating Kevin's hand. "Maybe they'll give us something free for bringing Humans."

The old doorman nodded approvingly when he saw that Kevin was carrying the stone tablet in a proper holder. Dorothy asked their host, "Why do you even have a contract bag?"

"It's a newlywed thing. Once you've been married for a while, everybody can tell just by looking at you together, but we never would have made it through the door of the honeymoon hotel without one."

Barzee kept Dorothy at her side, now quizzing the girl about human behaviors as depicted in the Grenouthian documentaries. Kevin went back to practicing his limited Frunge on the children, who impressed by his tenacity, began giving him the correct names for the things he pointed at. Most of the long walk took place in a sort of covered mall which their guide had chosen to limit exposure to the red sun for her guests. The children were just starting to get hungry for real, when they turned a corner and were nearly blinded by a dazzling chromium storefront.

"It can't be," Dorothy said.

"Human Burger," Barzee announced, as proudly as if she had opened the restaurant herself. "I'll bet it's just like home for you."

"It doesn't look very busy," Kevin commented.

"We're between mealtimes. I told the children to have a light breakfast to save room for frozen food."

"They bring in frozen food from Earth?" Dorothy asked hopefully. "That would be great."

The children rushed the counter, where a young man wearing a hat that looked like raw steak waited behind the register.

"We brought Humans," the shorter shrub declared.

"It's about time," the young man addressed the newcomers over the heads of the Frunge children. "We've been expecting two new fry cooks and a half-a-dozen waitstaff. Which are you?"

"Uh, customers?" Dorothy responded.

"Why?" The counterman pointed at the menu items etched in chrome, which Kevin and Dorothy had trouble reading through the glare. "Even though the Frunge can eat our dairy products, we use local sources for almost everything on the menu. It's human style, not human food."

"Oh, I'm so sorry," Barzee said. "Isn't there anything here you can eat yourselves?"

"There's the canned fruit salad," the young man replied. "Personally, I prefer ordering off the synthesized menu at the place across the street. What can I get you kids?"

"Ice cream," they screamed together.

"Two ice creams, coming up."

"Why can't we have that?" Dorothy asked.

The counterman held a metal cup under a machine that produced a thick slurry of what appeared to be frozen raw meat. After finishing it with a practiced twist of the wrist which left a little spiral peak on top, he asked the shrubs, "Do you want sprinkles on that?"

"Yes," they cried enthusiastically, and the counterman used what looked like an antique pepper grinder to deposit colorfully dyed bone chips over the frozen meat slush.

"I think we'll stick with the fruit salad," Kevin said.

Twelve

"Did you catalog anything interesting today?" Vivian asked, hopping up on the counter of the lost and found.

Samuel shrugged. "The Grenouthian who worked the shift before me shelved everything before she left. I'd ask Libby to change my schedule so I could come in after the lazy Drazen kid, but with all the different clocks on the station, it's not that simple."

"At least you have plenty of time for homework. It is a work/study job, after all."

"I finished all of my homework at home this week. I still haven't filled in the time from dropping our dance practice, and with Mom and Dorothy gone, it's really quiet. What did you bring?"

"My Dynastic Studies homework. I try to keep a few days ahead on everything, but we have a competency exam tomorrow so I can always use the extra preparation. Do you want to quiz me?"

"What do I know about Dynastic Studies?"

"A lot, unless you've been tuning me out whenever I tell you about my classes. Just use my notes and make up questions. The exam theme is contrasting the differences in property law implementation as practiced by the tunnel network species."

"All right," Samuel said. He accepted the proffered tab and skimmed a few pages. "Detail the main difference

between the Dollnick and Vergallian versions of *usufruct,*
but first, explain to me what it means."

"*Usufruct?* It's just *usus fructus,* you know? Use of the
fruit."

"Give me an example."

"Say we got married…" Vivian began.

"You're not even fifteen yet," he cut her off.

"Not tomorrow, in like five years or something. I'll be
super rich because my mom will give me part of her share
of the business. Now think of InstaSitter as an orchard,
where the business is the trees and the profits are the
fruits. As my husband, your rights will be limited to *usus
fructus.*"

"How about selling?"

"Can't do it. That would be abusive, *abusus.* But there's a
big difference between the way the Dollnicks and the
Vergallians practice *usufruct.* Can you tell me what it is?"

"You know, you sound more and more like Libby these
days," the boy grumbled.

"The Dollnicks live in a rigid patriarchic culture while
the Vergallians live in a matriarchic culture. So the property rights of a Dollnick wife or heiress are limited by
usufruct in the same way the property rights of a Vergallian
husband or heir are conscribed. Same idea, different
target."

"So how is what you said about InstaSitter different
from the Vergallian approach?"

"Because you'd be married to me, not my brother," Vivian explained. "In Vergallian culture, males can't inherit
income-producing property, and the opposite is true with
the Dollnicks."

"That's not very fair. So if you're born the wrong sex,
you end up with nothing?"

"No, you end up with *usus fructus*, which is the whole point. Say I was a Vergallian and we got married. If I died first, you wouldn't inherit, but you'd still have the income from whatever part of InstaSitter I left you for as long as you lived. The rest would be divided by our children, but the boys would only have *usus fructus* over their share."

"That doesn't make any sense. What if our daughters sold their share to somebody who wrecked the business? That would leave our sons with nothing."

"That's the problem with the model, which is why almost all of the dynastic families on the tunnel network practice some form of entailment."

"That sounds familiar. I think entailment is part of the plot in that book my mom is always talking about with Dring."

"What do they say about it?"

"I kind of tune it out," the boy admitted. "I got the impression that men and women could both inherit, but differently."

"It was probably set in a time and place where they practiced primogeniture," Vivian surmised. "Some cultures are so focused on preserving property and position that pretty much everything goes to the oldest son, like the Dollnick clans, or the oldest daughter, like with the Vergallians. With humans who practiced primogeniture, if there wasn't a son to inherit, then the estate got split up between the girls, and they all lost status."

"How do you know that?"

"My first assignment in this class was to contrast human inheritance traditions with those of the other tunnel network species, so I had to do a lot of reading about the history of property laws on Earth. You wouldn't believe the questions I got at the end of my presentation. A bunch of the alien students had their facts about humans all mixed up from watching documentaries. They were sure that human heirs were always burned at the funeral and the government took everything."

"A Vergallian queen once tried to sign my dad up to be her sacrificial king," Samuel said. "If he hadn't got killed in battle, they would have burned him."

"They have a lot of whacky codicils in their family contracts. A couple of Vergallian students presented, and one of them was a girl who is fourth in line for her family's throne, but only if she marries a guy with blonde hair who is at least a head taller than her."

"Is she Fleet? It's hard to imagine an Imperial family letting a heiress that high up in the line of succession run off to a Stryx station and attend the Open University."

"She's not Fleet, she just doesn't like blonde guys, and she's already the tallest Vergallian female I've ever met. The poor girl said she'd rather work as a hostess in a dance bar than have children who couldn't walk through a normal doorway without braining themselves. I guess a lot of Vergallian royal families have aesthetics codicils in their succession contracts, but just going for height generation after generation is bound to lead to health problems."

"Did you figure out how it works for the Drazens? With my mom away, my dad let me sit in on a poker game last week when a couple of the players were late. Herl was trying to explain to your dad how consortium ownership passed through families, but it seemed really complicated."

"Consortiums are funny because they require active participation, and how do you inherit a career? Say we were Drazens and we got married…"

"How come all of your examples start with us getting married?" Samuel protested.

"It just makes it more real," Vivian justified herself. "Abstractions are for lawyers. Do you want me to say, 'Imagine the party of the first part enters into a state of matrimony with the party of the second part?'"

"All right, say we're married Drazens."

"And say InstaSitter was a consortium, where my mom and Aunt Chastity were the primary stakeholders. My mom couldn't just give me, say, twenty-five percent of her holding, unless I starting doing a quarter of her work."

"Really? But what if you already had a job?"

"That's where you come in. As my husband, you could take over twenty-five percent of my mom's workload, and the other stakeholders would all accept that."

"Say your mom didn't have any children and she wanted to retire."

"Then she'd have to find somebody else to do her work, and maintaining her income would depend on that person's performance. Since you can't control what somebody else is going to do, and since it's hard to find a replacement who sings well enough to get approval for a high administrative position in a Drazen consortium, stakeholders without a family member willing to replace them usually sell out."

"So somebody else buys their stake and takes over the job, like the Dollnicks sell commissions in their military?"

"I think that's pretty rare because consortiums prefer to promote from within. From what I understood, the buyout payments are usually designed as pensions, a variable share of the profit depending on external factors."

"You mean, even though your mom and aunt founded InstaSitter and built it into what it is today, if it was a

Drazen consortium and one of them retired without a replacement from the family, all of their equity would be converted into an uncertain royalty stream that died with them?"

Vivian looked at Samuel in surprise. "You really have been paying attention when I talk about business, haven't you? From the standpoint of the major stakeholders, it seems unfair, but all of the small stakeholders celebrate when a founding family lets go. It's how the Drazens redistribute wealth without wars or economic collapses."

"What do the other species think of it?"

"The Dollnicks and Vergallians obviously think that the Drazens are nuts. The Hortens actually practice something similar to the consortium structure for large businesses, and the Frunge are somewhere between the two groups."

"What about the older species, the Grenouthians and the Verlocks?"

"The Grenouthians organize everything along family lines, but they also give points in their enterprises to whoever contributes the most to making them successful. And they pool a lot of their family wealth, so everybody ends up with something. The Verlocks pay a ton of taxes to their emperor, but the emperor is required by law to spend it all on public welfare, most of which is funneled through their academies."

"So say we were married Grenouthians and your mom had a point in their news network.

"A point in the entire network, not just one show? She'd be incredible wealthy, like a Stryx librarian or something."

"I meant could she sell it, or give you a quarter of the point, and could I spend all of that income forever without having to do anything?"

"Oh, you're back to *usus fructus*. I don't really know how it works with the bunnies because they're kind of secretive. We have twelve of them in the class and nobody knows their names, so we just refer to them by numbers." Vivian pointed at the tab that the boy was still holding. "Ask me something else now. Property law isn't just about rights and inheritance."

Samuel took another minute to skim forward. "Okay. Contrast the concept of private property in the old Gem Empire versus the new."

"Ugh, you had to pick that one? Other than small personal items, the clones didn't have private property in their old empire. Everything was owned by the sisters in common, but the elites had access to consumable goods that the peons could only dream of."

"And?"

"That's the hard part. Since they overthrew the elites and started cloning other members of their species from the samples they bought off the Farlings, the whole society is sort of waiting to see what happens. They're talking about distributing some of the commonly held property to individuals, but their old society was so geared to cloning that they don't have a lot of normal stuff."

"What do you mean?"

"All of the other tunnel network species have extensive land holdings for farming because nobody eats synthesized food by choice. Nobody except the Gem, who shut down their agricultural sector in favor of factory produced food that was supposed to be perfect. But what's the point of distributing a billionth of a percent of a cloning facility or food factory to the local Gem? They can feed and clothe themselves, but for hundreds of generations their entire economy was based on cloning more Gem, and they can't replace that overnight."

"How about apartments or housing?"

"Even the elites lived in shared housing, it was just more luxurious than the worker dormitories. And the workers all had roommates, so what would you do with a quarter of a room or a half of a bunk bed? They're trying to move in the direction of a time-based currency system, where you bank the time you work and will eventually be able to spend it on community products."

"They could buy stuff from the other species."

"With what money? They were pretty isolated the last ten or twenty thousand years. The other species buy some of the nanobot technology that they developed primarily for spying purposes, but that's about it."

"So they're in worse shape than humans, even."

"Well, I wouldn't go that far. Most of their technology isn't up to that of the other advanced species, but they've had faster-than-light drives for a couple of hundred thousand years. It's just that they spent all their energy fighting each other and then cloning the winner."

"I've never heard it put so succinctly," a new voice spoke from behind Vivian, who almost fell off the counter.

"Sorry, I didn't see you come in," Samuel said to the clone. "Did you lose something?"

"A great deal of self esteem, though it's reassuring to hear that we aren't at the absolute bottom of the heap. But I came looking for my spare double boiler. Our cooperative catered a picnic event for Humans last cycle, and I'm afraid my clean-up crew grew tipsy drinking wine from unfinished glasses and somehow left it behind during the cleanup. I didn't notice it was missing until we had two events that needed a double boiler at the same time yesterday."

"What's a double boiler?" Samuel asked.

The clone and the girl exchanged a universal eye roll over the ignorance of men.

"How else would you melt chocolate for dipping strawberries?" the Gem demanded.

"Oh. So it's like a crock pot?"

"You explain it to him," the clone said to Vivian.

"It's a pot with an insert so you get uniform heat and the chocolate doesn't separate," the girl said. "We have a Frunge one that can also be used as two separate pots, but Grandma just puts a glass bowl directly in water, brings it to a simmer, and then turns off the heat. She claims it's better than a double boiler."

"Really?" the caterer asked.

"Grandma says that slower is always better with chocolate, and she doesn't even stir it."

"Is it this?" Samuel called from a shelving unit, where he had located two stainless steel pots that seemed to be stuck together.

The cloned glanced over and answered with an impatient, "Yes, yes," before turning back to Vivian. "Does your grandmother know other chocolate secrets? I'd be willing to pay for the information."

"No, she's more into working with odd alien ingredients that we can eat after baking. She makes really good Thorian spice tarts."

"Who are the Thorians?"

"They aren't on the tunnel network, but sometimes their stuff shows up in the Shuk. Even though they aren't oxygen breathers, they export some weird spices and stuff that aren't poisonous to us when properly prepared."

143

"Thank you, young lady. I intend to try your grand-mother's technique, but it's good to have my double boiler back."

"Hold on, I have to remove it from inventory," Samuel said, placing the pots on the turntable. "Double boiler from location PS 109/103 claimed by Gem caterer."

After the clone left, Samuel picked up the girl's tab again and skimmed a little further through her notes. "How do the property rights of artificial people differ from those of the species they are modeled on?"

"They're the same, at least on the tunnel network," Vivian qualified her answer. "I don't know how enforceable their rights are where the Stryx aren't watching everything."

"Does that include body mortgages?"

"What about them?"

"Artificial people usually need them to get started in life, at least, human-created AI does."

"So? A mortgage is a mortgage. Plenty of people have them, though I suppose with the advanced species, it usually takes the form of a family or clan loan."

"But we're not talking about a spaceship or a house. It's their bodies."

"I know you're used to seeing Thomas and Chance in their current bodies, but those are really just machines, right? Their minds are what matter."

"But their minds can't exist without the machines."

"I don't know if that's true. Libby? Can artificial people exist without machines?"

"They can be stored, but they need a system capable of processing their instructions to maintain sentience, and physicality is sometimes linked to consciousness," the Stryx librarian responded.

"But it's different with Jeeves and his body, right?" Samuel followed up.

"Stryx aren't on the exam," Vivian said.

"Why not? They're a tunnel network species."

"Thank you for including us, Samuel," Libby said. "It's true that although young Stryx inhabit a physical body, they aren't dependent on it for sentience, and most of their consciousness resides...elsewhere. The property concern you raised is valid, but I can assure you that in the tens of millions of years that the Stryx have offered body mortgages to newly sentient AI, we have never foreclosed."

"Then why does Chance tell all those stories about hiding out off the tunnel network when she stopped making payments?" Vivian asked.

"Chance was hiding from her conscience, not the repo man."

"Other than the body mortgages, are there property rights differences for artificial people and their species?" Samuel asked the librarian.

"Theoretically, no, but issues surrounding inheritance arise with all types of AI who live in systems run by biologicals."

"Why's that?"

"If an artificial person came to Union Station a hundred thousand years from now and claimed to be the offspring of Thomas and Chance, it would be easy for me or any other Stryx who knew the parents to verify the relation with a consensual scan. Otherwise, for AI to establish a line of descent requires registrations and recordkeeping."

"You mean there's no simple DNA test for relatives, like the way the Farling doctor found my dad's long-lost sister," Vivian said.

"Precisely. Because artificial people live in manufactured bodies which are often engineered by species other than those who created them, their identity must be established in other ways. For example, the artificial Sharf use closely guarded cryptographic systems and one-time keys to establish their rights. But the infrastructure and recordkeeping required for authentication is only available in Sharf space."

Vivian dismissed the subject with, "Sharf aren't on the exam either."

Thirteen

The studio audience applause was thunderous, and Aisha finally understood why her producer had insisted on making her return from maternity leave into the first extended-length special for the show. Between foot-stamping Hortens, whistling Drazens, and belly-slapping Grenouthians, she gave up trying to begin her prepared speech several times, and even had to turn her face from the front camera to wipe away a few tears. After five minutes, the crowd finally settled down, allowing Aisha to speak.

"Thank you all for..." she began, but was drowned out by another deafening greeting. This second round of applause was just a form of alien good manners, and stopped as abruptly as it started.

"Thank you, thank you. As you know, I've been out on maternity leave following the birth of my son, Steve, who we named after my mother-in-law's father."

"Let's see the offspring!" an alien shouted, and the rest of the audience took up the chant.

Fenna, who was in the front row of seats holding her baby brother, stood up turned around so everybody could see the little boy in his blue fleece jumpsuit, with Dollnick noise-cancelling earmuffs hiding half of his face. The girl took one of his little hands and waved it, causing the more susceptible aliens to launch into their equivalent of baby-talk praise.

Aisha waited for all of the cooing, trilling, and lip vibrating to exhaust itself before continuing. "I want to take a moment to thank the substitute hosts who filled in while I was on leave. During the last two cycles, Dzally showed us that she has a heart of gold, and I'm sure you all agree that she deserves her own show."

Another round of applause rocked the studio, and the Frunge present began chanting, "Dzally! Dzally!"

"And Shola's gift for communicating with children made her time on the show a blessing for all of us."

The Hortens all stamped their feet in appreciation, and the rest of the audience applauded politely.

"Finally, I want to apologize for Jeeves," Aisha said. "I know that the ratings for the shows he hosted were through the roof, but I'm afraid that the activities he introduced weren't age appropriate, even though I'm sure that the children were never in real danger."

"Bring back the 'Spiral Slide of Death!'" a younger member of the audience cried out.

"That's exactly the sort of…" Aisha began, but out of the corner of her eye she saw the assistant director making the 'move it along' gesture, and reined herself in. "Today we have a special guest from a new species. Her family has just arrived on the station with an invited delegation to consider membership in the tunnel network, so let's all be on our best behavior. We're also beginning the final cast rotation for one of your all-time favorite groups, so let's give a big 'Let's Make Friends' welcome back for Orsilla, Vzar, Clume, Spinner, Pluck, Krolyohne and Mike."

The audience responded enthusiastically, and the children entered the set one by one. The Grenouthian engineer in the booth projected a hologram over each of the cast members, displaying a brief bio of their time on the show. Orsilla carried a bouquet of flowers, which she presented to the host with a formal curtsey.

"Thank you so much for the flowers," Aisha said. "It's very thoughtful of you."

"The producer gave them to me backstage," the Horten girl replied. "Your baby is so cute. Can we play with him?"

"Maybe after the show. Has everybody been well the last six cycles?"

"I guess," Orsilla replied, and the other children all chipped in with similar noncommittal responses.

"And how is school?"

"Hard," the aliens chorused, but Mike and Spinner both said "Fun," at the same time, drawing envious looks from the others.

"Why don't we all share what we learned while we were away from the show. Pluck?"

"I don't know," the Drazen boy replied with a shrug.

"Krolyohne?"

"Infinite dimensional vector space," the Verlock girl responded.

"Oh. I don't exactly know what it is, but it sounds interesting," Aisha said. "How about you, Clume?"

"Zero-G fabrication techniques," the eight-year-old Dollnick replied. "I liked the cold welding part, but I had trouble with galling."

"You need to avoid sliding the pieces together," the young Stryx advised him.

"Orsilla?" Aisha prompted.

"I tried to replicate the results of a Human experiment using white rats in a maze for my alien psychology elective."

"Aren't you a little young to be studying alien psychology?"

"That's why the teacher made me do Humans. You're so simple."

"Did you succeed?"

"No, but I got top marks for methodology. I determined that either the rats or the Humans must have cheated in the original experiments."

"And how about you, Spinner?" Aisha asked, prepared to hear the usual answer about multiverse math.

"I learned how to change diapers," the Stryx said proudly. "Fenna taught me on Steve."

"Did she teach Mike too?"

"He wouldn't even try. He said it was gross."

"Vzar?"

"I sintered molybdenum," the Frunge boy said, picking an achievement that would most impress his schoolmates.

"Really?" Orsilla asked skeptically.

"Well, I was there, and I watched the temperature readout," Vzar said.

"Either way it sounds fun," Aisha said. "How about you, Mike?"

"I helped my grandpa in the Shuk," the boy said. "I want to sell stuff when I grow up."

"I thought you wanted to be a pirate," Spinner reminded him.

"I grew out of that," Mike said. "Besides, Grandpa says there's more money in retail."

"Well, it sounds like everybody learned something new, except for Pluck," Aisha summed up. "Are you sure you can't think of anything?"

"I learned how to play the harp," the Drazen boy admitted.

150

"Boys don't play harp," the Horten girl said dismissively.

"Orsilla!" Aisha scolded her. "Music is a wonderful gift, and the instruments don't know who's playing them."

"Our instruments do," Krolyohne interjected.

"I only started learning because my aunt left the station and we needed a harpist for the family ensemble," Pluck said. "As soon as my younger sister's tentacle is long enough, I'm changing to percussion."

"I won't be a bit surprised if when the time comes, you find that you've fallen in love with the harp and decide to stay with it," Aisha predicted. Pluck just made a face in response.

"What did you learn during your maternity leave?" Spinner asked the host.

"Did you see the Snorinth actually bring your baby?" Clume added.

"Snorinths don't bring Human babies," Pluck said. "They come in baskets carried by a giant bird, just like Drazens."

"Who ever heard of babies getting delivered by birds?" Orsilla said scornfully.

"Well, where do Horten babies come from then?" the Drazen challenged her.

"My mother and father fasted and prayed to Gortunda, and then I appeared in a shoebox," Orsilla replied confidently, though the titter from the studio audience made her wonder if her parents hadn't been entirely truthful. "Where do Verlock babies come from, Krolyohne?"

"We're shaped from lava and then our parents blow into our mouths until we start breathing," the Verlock girl said. "That's why my mommy lost so much weight after my little brother arrived. She held her breath for cycles and cycles to make sure she would have enough, and it made her belly stick out."

"So if a Snorinth didn't bring your baby, who did?" the Dollnick child asked Aisha.

"Uh, Pluck was right," Aisha said, acutely conscious of her eight-year-old daughter sitting in the front row. "A giant bird brought Steve in a basket."

"So why were you so fat before your vacation?" Orsilla challenged her.

"I was holding my breath to help the poor stork take off after bringing the baby," Aisha improvised. "They get very tired so they need the extra boost to get airborne again. Oh, it's time for an announcement from our sponsors, but we'll be right back with our new friend."

The status light on the front immersive camera winked out, and Aisha took the flowers over to the mantle above the set's fireplace, pretending she couldn't hear the follow-on questions about babies. A relative of the show's producer who was listed on the payroll as a 'fourth grip' led a young Alt onto the stage. The girl rushed around giving each of the alien children a hug, including Spinner, but avoided Mike, saving the boy from an embarrassing smooch. Then the assistant director counted them back in, and Aisha launched into the second segment of the show.

"Today our special guest is Meena, from the newly discovered Alt species. You have a very pretty name, Meena. Does it mean anything?"

"It's a type of gnat," the girl replied cheerfully.

"Oh, how interesting. Do the Alts commonly name their children after bugs?"

"And fish, and trees, and animals, and flowers," Meena listed on her fingers. "And rivers, and mountains, and birds, and…"

"Your people must honor nature," Orsilla cut her off.

"We do! You're so smart to see that right away."

"The other children have just returned to the show after a long break," Aisha told the Alt girl. "Right before you came on we were discussing what they learned since we last saw them. Have you learned anything recently that you'd like to share?"

"I've been studying asymptotic series for numerical methods," Meena said enthusiastically. "My mom tutors me."

"That's advanced for a Human your age," Krolyohne rumbled.

"Meena may look human or Vergallian, but she's from a different species," Aisha reminded the children.

"I think her head is larger than a Human's," Clume observed. He raised his lower set of arms with the hands spread apart and peered at Mike between them. At the same time, he held up his upper set of arms with the hands spread so he could visually measure Meena's head for comparison. "Yup. Maybe ten percent more volume?"

"She smells a lot like a Human, but better," Pluck said, sniffing the air.

"Grab my hands and push," Vzar demanded. The Alt girl obligingly pitted herself against the Frunge boy, and after a few seconds, he said, "Stronger than Humans too."

"But can she do this?" Mike demanded, putting his thumb to his nose and wiggling his fingers at the girl.

"Mike!" Aisha exclaimed. "Where are your manners? Tell Meena that you're sorry."

"It's my fault," the Alt girl said. "I should have hugged him, but he scares me a little."

"Mike scares you?"

"He didn't do anything bad," Meena rushed to correct herself. "It's just like, you know, if you hear a dog growling in the dark, and even though you know that dogs are good, you don't want to go that way?"

Aisha found the alien girl's honesty strangely disconcerting, but she remembered suffering from a similar fear when she was a child. "I think the best way to get over our fears is to play a game together. Do you have any Alt games you could teach us?"

"Most of our games are for a family," Meena replied. She bit her lower lip and thought for a moment. "I know. We can play Deretz."

"What's that?" Vzar asked.

"Everybody sits in a circle and you have to say something really nice about the person next to you."

"I like the sound of that," Aisha said enthusiastically, gracefully seating herself on the floor. "Would you go first to show us how to play?"

The children all followed the host's lead and began arranging themselves in a circle on the floor of the set. The Alt girl moved as if she planned to sit next to Mike, but then she chickened out and managed to put Orsilla between herself and the human.

"So we always play to the left," Meena said, and turned to face Clume. "You're so strong and well put-together. I wish I had four arms like you do."

"Thank you," Clume said, the first time Aisha could ever remember hearing the words escape the Dollnick child. He turned to his left and addressed the Verlock girl. "If I could do math like you, I'd drop out of school and start building space stations."

"I'm not so smart," Krolyohne protested, embarrassed by the praise. She turned to the young Stryx who floated by her other side. "Spinner is the real genius. And you're so generous to make time for helping us learn when you could be exploring the multiverse."

"Thank you," the young Stryx squeaked, running all of his case lights into the red end of the visible spectrum to simulate blushing. He spun around a few times, and stopped facing Aisha.

"You treat me like one of the family even though I'm not from a biological species. You're my favorite grown-up."

"Thank you, Spinner. That's so kind. And I couldn't wish better friends for my daughter than you and Mike." The host turned to address the young Frunge who sat on her left. "You've never complained even once about anything on the show, even though I know the lighting must be hard on your hair vines. I think you're a very fine boy."

Vzar mumbled something polite under his breath and turned to Pluck.

"You're okay for a Drazen, even if you do play the harp."

"Whatever," Pluck replied, turning to Mike. "You come up with cool rules when we play games, even though Orsilla always changes them."

"I know," Mike said. Then he turned reluctantly to face the Horten girl, who always seemed to take the opposite side any time he ventured an opinion. An inspired thought hit him and he told her, "You're really pretty," laughing inside as he set the trap.

"Thank you," Orsilla replied. "I didn't know you were capable of such insight." She turned to the Alt girl, completing the circle. "You could be a nurse or a kindergarten teacher, you're so nice."

"Do you really mean that?" Meena asked, and she impulsively hugged the Horten girl. Then she turned to Clume, and said, "When I turn off the translation device the show staff gave me and listen to your speech, it sounds like birds singing."

Clume was so shocked by this compliment that he sat with his mouth open. Mike took the opportunity to ask, "How do we win this game?"

"Everybody wins," the Alt girl replied, looking puzzled. "If you run out of nice things to say, you can ask for help from the others."

"So when does it end?" Pluck asked.

"We can play for hours and hours back home, but then somebody gets called for a meal or chores, and we have to stop."

A snort came from outside of the set, and Aisha looked over to see the assistant director miming falling asleep and hanging himself at the same time. "I think it's a lovely game, but we probably don't want to overdo it," she said. "I heard that you've never seen our show before. Is that right, Meena?"

"Yes. Am I doing something wrong?"

"No, you're the perfect guest. I just realized that you probably don't know our song, and I don't want you to feel left out at the end of the show when we all sing. I think there's just enough time left before the next commercial to teach it to you with the help of the other children."

"I'd like that very much."

"Pluck?" Aisha asked, giving the boy an encouraging look.

"*Don't be a stranger because I look funny,*" the Drazen sang.

"But you don't look funny," Meena reassured him. "I wish I had six fingers and a tentacle."

"It's the first line of the song," Pluck told her.

"Oh, that's why you were singing. You have a lovely voice."

"Spinner?" Aisha prompted.

"*You look weird to me, but let's make friends,*" the Stryx sang.

"I look weird to you?" Meena asked, hugging herself. "I know I'm not metallic, so I guess that makes sense. Would you feel better if I wrapped myself in foil?"

"It's the second line of our song," Aisha reminded her, becoming a little frustrated with the Alt girl's exaggerated sensitivity.

"Right. I won't forget again."

"Orsilla?" Aisha prompted.

"*I'll give you a tissue if your nose is runny,*" the Horten girl sang.

"You would? Thank you. Look," Meena said, opening her own little handbag. "I also carry tissues to give people, and cough drops. Plus these tweezers, for if somebody gets a splinter."

"You're incredibly nice," the Horten girl couldn't help saying. "Are all Alt girls like you?"

"I think so. My friend Halla carries Pitto beans to give the other children, even though she doesn't like them herself, and Dintill carries bandages that her mom draws little pictures on. I pretended I hurt my finger just to get one because they're so pretty," Meena admitted.

"Mike?" Aisha asked.

"What did I do?"

"Tell her the last line of the song," Orsilla said.

"I'm as scared as you, so let's make friends," the boy half sang, half mumbled.

Meena stared at him and her eyes began to tear up. "That's so beautiful. Who wrote this song?" she asked Aisha.

"Uh, I worked on it with Libby, our station librarian, so the lyrics rhyme in all the tunnel network languages."

"They rhyme in Alt too."

"They do?" Aisha asked in surprise. "How is that possible?"

"And we're out," the assistant director said. "It's a long break, so feel free to get up and stretch." He hopped up onto the set and pulled Aisha aside. "Listen. I know this is your comeback special and everything, but the director and the producer are both in my ear about your guest."

"Isn't she perfect?"

"Perfectly boring. She can stay on the set, but don't ask her any more questions or we're going to run a test of the emergency station evacuation system."

"I've never even heard of that."

"Neither had I until the producer told me about it. It's just a loud tone and an animation artist's conception of the station blowing apart."

Fourteen

"So what's the difference between what you're doing and industrial espionage?" Kevin asked Dorothy as they shuffled through the docking arm of the Chintoo orbital with their magnetic cleats activated for Zero-G.

"Industrial espionage is like aliens spying on each other to steal technological secrets," the girl replied. "The whole point of fashion design is for your clothes to be seen and appreciated."

"But aren't we here because your competitors will be showing fashions that haven't launched yet?"

"We're here so I can meet Ug, the Sharf artificial person whose group does our manufacturing."

"If your clothes are manufactured on Chintoo, why are you and Flazint always sewing little bits onto stuff?"

"Little bits onto stuff! I know you aren't really interested in women's clothes, but you could at least pretend to listen. I pay attention when you talk about ship mainte-nance with my Dad and Paul."

"No you don't." Kevin said, his voice starting high on the first word, dropping for the second, and splitting the difference for the third.

Dorothy stopped in front of the open safety hatch at the end of the pressurized spoke and pulled her arms in tight against her sides, her wrists crossed over her chest. Kevin sighed and picked her up by the elbows, then gently tossed her feet-first through the opening. Her cleats stuck to the opposite wall, where she waited impatiently for him to arrive so they could resume the argument, albeit in a new orientation.

"Anyway, we do all of the customization for our bespoke line on the station," Dorothy continued. "Flazint and I both enjoy working with our hands, but we have aliens all over the station doing piece work at home."

"Affie doesn't like sewing?"

"She hates it. And even though Affie's really good at math, she doesn't like to work on marketing strategy or any of the other business stuff because it reminds her too much of royal training. She's really just into art and hanging out. Flazint says we're lucky that she has such a laid-back boyfriend or we'd never see her."

"Stick? I don't think that guy even has a job."

"He sells—never mind. The point is that Jeeves wants me to get more involved in strategy. He's supposed to be the Stryx expert on the human psyche, but he admits that he just doesn't get young women."

"So your idea of strategy is to sneak around Chintoo looking at new designs from your competitors to find out what teenage girls are thinking? We'll have to go back to the ship and get spacesuits then, because most of this place is open to the vacuum."

Dorothy pivoted gracefully and punched Kevin in the shoulder without even slowing. "I knew you weren't listening when I told you that there's a job fair going on. You kept saying, 'Yeah, I get it,' but you were really playing that Frunge maglev game."

"Those are going to sell big to the Vergallians. Games like that are just the sort of thing that slips in under the tech ban because they don't have any practical application. Besides, I got them for a song."

"No, you got them on the Frunge elevator hub for that weird metal powder you bartered for on the Drazen station. And the fact that the Drazen woman sang when you closed that deal tells me that you gave her too much."

"She was happy to get all of those blank Horten holocubes I traded for back on Union Station. The Drazens and the Hortens have some kind of feud going, so you can always turn a cred selling stuff from one species to the other."

"Go on," Dorothy said with an exaggerated groan.

"Go on what?"

"I know you want to tell me what you traded to get the holocubes."

"Just some Horten e-rations from one of the ships in Paul's collection. You know he's not really into bartering, so he gives me the little stuff like that to dispose of and we split fifty-fifty."

"What is Paul going to do with blank holocubes?"

"Record home holograms. They're the permanent kind, not the one-shots, so lots of species use them for baby tricks."

"Right. And when we get to Ailia's world with those maglev toys, what are you going to trade them for?"

"Horten e-rations," Kevin replied earnestly, and then dodged out of the way before Dorothy could punch him again. "Besides, I was just teasing about the spacesuits. I knew why we're here. Chintoo only has one large biological-friendly space for fairs and that's where we're headed. Did you see that spherical section during our approach?"

"I shut my eyes after we almost hit that hazmat dumping arm," Dorothy said. "How can an AI traffic controller be so bad at docking a ship?"

"Chintoo inhabitants have a love/hate relationship with biologicals. The artificial people and AI come here because they want to get away from the species that created them, but they don't have a lot of material needs, so biologicals provide most of their business."

"If they don't need stuff, why work so hard to make money?"

"I guess they just like to keep busy, and you never know when money will come in handy. Anyway, that's the entrance just ahead, so what should I expect?"

"It's a job fair. The message Jeeves sent me said that this is the main one on Chintoo for the new fashion manufacturing season, and I've never been before."

"Jeeves wants you to get an undercover job as a fashion spy? What about our companionship contract? I own you for another five cycles."

"You've got the ownership bit backwards, and I'm not here for a job. Businesses that have products they want mass manufactured at low cost show the prototypes at these job fairs. The artificial people and AIs who live on Chintoo bid on the work. I thought you'd been here a bunch of times."

"Just to pick up factory seconds and overruns. I never knew they held job fairs to get work."

"Wait. You come here to buy defective merchandise and leftovers from large orders? I'm pretty sure those are all supposed to be recycled or destroyed."

"No wonder they're such a good deal. Hey, don't look at the central light orb or you'll be blinded."

162

Dorothy squinted up at the tiny artificial sun that provided the light and heat in the Chintoo exhibition hall, and managed to say, "It's really bright," before Kevin put a hand on the back of her head and forced her gaze down.

"I don't want to spend the next six hours describing dresses to you because you can't see. Wow, there's some really weird stuff on display."

"None of that is for humanoids," Dorothy told him. "We can check it out after looking at the good stuff." She started right up the spherical deck towards a section that was dominated by Horten designers, and then pulled Kevin close to whisper, "See that yellow lady showing a handbag to the AI with all the metal tentacles?"

"Hard to miss."

"I recognize those bags. The Hortens market them as handmade."

"Maybe they're handmade by artificial people."

"It's still cheating. I'm kind of surprised I don't see more Vergallian designers here," she added.

"Think of all of their tech-ban worlds. I bet they have tens of millions of women doing piece work on every one. Most of the Vergallian trade goods are handmade."

"Oooh, look at those sashes." Dorothy shuffled off rapidly on her magnetic cleats towards the display where a Horten designer was demonstrating to a skeptical artificial person how the long silky bands could be wound around a torso to create different looks.

The Horten woman glanced up at the newcomer and demanded bluntly, "Who are you with?"

"I'm just looking."

"I know you're just looking. I want to know who you work for so I can keep an eye on your catalog for copies. It's only fair."

The artificial person looked on in amusement as Dorothy struggled to come up with an answer.

"I'm not going to bite you, honey," the Horten continued. "Just look around. This place is crawling with fashion designers."

"Oh, I wondered why there were so many biologicals," Dorothy said. "I work for SBJ Fashions. We're mainly on the stations."

"I've heard of you. Somebody gave me one of your hats as a gift. Is the young man with you?"

"We have a companionship contract but we left it on the ship," Dorothy replied defensively before realizing that the Horten wasn't interested in her lifestyle. "He's just a trader."

The Horten nodded and turned back to the Sharf artificial person. "Look, 21F9ku73. I know this can't be first time somebody designed a dress that requires a reusable adhesive strip. What's the problem?"

"Call me, 'Ku,' and I'm afraid you don't understand the physics. There must be a dozen different mechanisms holding the folds of your prototype together, including surface tension and static electricity. You may as well sell people boxes of the plastic cling film you all use for food preservation and tell them to wrap themselves in it."

"How about Velcro?" the Horten suggested, casting a guilty glance in Dorothy's direction.

"Human technology? Great in theory, but it's too noisy and you can't make it thin enough for an application like this. You'd be better off with their carbon-fiber reinforced elastomers. There was a group of scientists from Earth at our last polymer job fair showing a surprisingly useful adhesive system they want to have mass-manufactured. Apparently they copied it from lizard feet almost a century ago, but never quite managed to make it work outside of the lab."

The Horten beckoned the artificial person to step closer, and the conversation proceeded in whispers, leading Dorothy to toss her head in irritation and stalk off to the next display.

Kevin trailed behind, trying to figure out who would possibly wear the fashions on display. Like most traders, he had a professional interest in almost everything that could be bartered or sold, but his dealings in clothing had usually been limited to rugged coveralls for laborers and baby clothes, which went well everywhere. Then he realized that Dorothy had been standing in the same spot as if paralyzed for several minutes, and he shuffled forward up the inside of the giant sphere to see what was wrong.

"It's the future," she breathed in an awed voice, grabbing his arm with one hand and pointing with the other. "This changes everything."

"The Verlock with the little stick things? What are they, tent stakes?"

"They're heels, you idiot. Look at the hologram. They feature gyroscopic stabilizers that kick in at critical tipping points, a dynamically expandable base plate that automatically adjusts to the contact surface to prevent sinking in or punctures, and a memory metal matrix that offers continual adjustment through the full height range."

"Did you swallow a technical dictionary when I wasn't looking?"

"I'm serious. This is big. That guy isn't a fashion designer, he's just an inventor. According to the holo-presentation, his wife wanted to wear heels, but Verlocks

165

are so heavy that every alien shoe she tried either broke or popped a hole in the floor."

"This isn't the beginning of another diet thing, is it?"

"What's wrong with you? I want to get those heels for our new line. We won't just have the best looking and most comfortable shoes on the market, but they'll be the most technologically advanced as well."

"So what are you waiting for?" Kevin asked. "I'm sure the guy will be thrilled that somebody is interested in his invention."

"I'm nervous," Dorothy admitted. "It's like that once-in-a-lifetime deal you traders are always talking about. What if he doesn't like humans?"

"I'll talk to him."

"No, wait," the girl said, pulling back on his arm, and then letting it go. "Okay."

Kevin intentionally swallowed several mouthfuls of air as he approached the display, and then let out a rumbling burp, the closest he could come to approximating the Verlock greeting.

"Biological or artificial?" the inventor asked, minimizing his word count to avoid testing the potential customer's patience.

"Biological. Human. We're interested in acquiring a test batch of your heels for a new line of shoes under development at SBJ Fashions."

"Cost prohibitive," the Verlock stated honestly. "Handmade. Chintoo manufacturers uncertain."

"You mean you made all of these yourself and you haven't found a group that can mass manufacture them yet?"

"Magnetic monopoles, superconductors, nanogyroscopes," the Verlock replied, and his tone of despair survived the translation. "Complicated."

"Of course they're complicated," Dorothy entered the conversation. "It's a brilliant invention, and you can't let all these egghead engineers get you down."

"I'm an egghead engineer," the Verlock protested.

"Nonsense, you're an artist. If you can't find a manufacturing group here on Chintoo, I'm sure we can do something on Union Station, even if it does require hand assembly. I *must* have those heels!"

"Eighty Stryx cred a pair to manufacture," the Verlock groaned. "Who would buy? Long trip, no purpose."

"Are you kidding? Eighty creds is nothing. Well, it's something, but you talk to our guys here and we'll help with the financing. Has Ug bid on your job yet? I was supposed to ping him as soon as we got here, but I wanted to have a look around first."

"Ug. 34F9ug21?" the Verlock asked laboriously. "Eighty-seven creds, plus machining."

"He'll make you a deal if I tell him to. Trust me, you've got something great here. The gyroscopic stabilization alone is worth a hundred creds on the selling price. What do you think shoes sell for anyway?"

"Don't know. Wife shops."

"I can't believe these shoes haven't taken over the Verlock market at any price. I've never even seen one of your females wearing high heels."

"Uh, Dorothy?" Kevin said. "Maybe his wife is the only one who wants to wear heels. I imagine it's pretty uncomfortable for humanoids of their, er, proportions, to wear fancy shoes."

"Yes," the Verlock confirmed.

"You guys are dense," Dorothy said angrily, forgetting that the heavy alien would take it for a simple statement of fact. "If Verlock women don't wear high heels it's because they can't buy shoes that won't break. Comfort and safety just don't come into it." She pointed at her ear and stared off into space for a moment, which really meant looking at the floor a little higher up the curvature of the sphere. "I can't connect to the central exchange on this stupid orbital. How am I supposed to ping Ug?"

"Access with registration," the Verlock said. "I will contact 34F9ug21." After a long pause, he continued, "Ug will meet you in Corridor Two, Number Four. On the way."

"Don't go anywhere or sell your heels to anybody else," Dorothy commanded imperiously.

"I'll be waiting," the Verlock said to their departing backs. He wasn't at all insulted or surprised by the abrupt departure because he had seen enough Grenouthian documentaries to take strange alien behavior in stride. Besides, the Chintoo manufacturer had agreed to meet the girl without hesitation, saying something about a Stryx being a partner in the business.

Corridor Two turned out to be all the way around the other side of the sphere, and by the time the humans worked their way past the first three numbered spaces, a tall Sharf artificial person was already waiting for them in front of the fourth.

"SBJ Fashions?" he inquired in flawless English.

"Yes. I'm Dorothy and this is Kevin. I'm sure Jeeves has told you all about our trip."

"Enough," the Sharf said. "Forgive me for not inviting you back to our pod, but you aren't wearing spacesuits, and I'm not sure that all of my team are as liberal minded about provisional bonding contracts as the Frunge. Let's go in."

"In where?" the girl asked, looking away from the artificial Sharf to see where they were going. "Why isn't there a sign?"

"Signage on Chintoo consists of digital signals," the artificial Sharf replied. "Human Burger opened last cycle and I've been meaning to try it."

"Told you so," Dorothy muttered to Kevin. "They're going to ruin the whole galaxy."

"What can I do you for?" asked the cheerful artificial person behind the counter.

Ug's eye stalks waggled with humor when he saw the tinfoil hat worn by the clerk. "What do you suggest?"

"We have a wide array of fuels for micro-turbines, and harmonically flavored inductive chargers at the tables that are compatible with most power packs. There's a degaussing booth around the back, and if you choose any three items from the full menu, you get entered in our daily drawing for a free diagnostic test in the Chintoo clinic. In addition, your entry code is added to the random sequencer for one of three chances for a grand prize, an all-expenses-paid trip to Earth."

"Has anybody won one of grand prizes yet?" Kevin asked.

"Nobody has even bought three items from the menu, but we're making adjustments," the artificial person replied.

"I'll take a pure grain alcohol, plus whatever these two are ordering," Ug said.

"We'll have the fruit salad," Dorothy requested in a resigned voice.

The clerk's shoulders slumped. "We dropped that from the menu after two cycles because nobody ordered it. Unloaded the starter inventory on a trader."

169

"We'll just have water," Kevin said.

"I'm not sure we have any. Water isn't very popular with robots."

"It's on your mixers list," Ug pointed out. "Give us three alcohols and two H2O mixers."

The clerk grabbed a little silver hammer and dinged the bell which hung over the counter. "You've won a free diagnostic, plus you're entered for the grand prize. I'll bring your drinks right out to your table."

Ug froze for a moment when the data packet about the prize was forwarded to him by the register system. "Talk about making things unnecessarily complicated. If you printed these rules and conditions on a roll of paper, I could walk to Earth on it."

"You don't want to go anyway," Dorothy said, leading the way to the closest table. "Lots of particles in the air and acid rain. My friend, Chance, is an artificial person, and she wore a spacesuit outside when she went."

"Thanks for the warning. Jeeves said that you're in charge of new business development and I should offer my full cooperation. Drilyenth told me that you're interested in manufacturing his invention."

"Was that his name? I forgot to ask." Dorothy paused while the clerk deposited a small tray with five cut-crystal glasses on the table. "Those heels are a breakthrough product. You could put them on anything and it would be a smash hit. We have to get them."

"My rough estimate was forty thousand creds for the machining setup, and eight-seven creds a pair at quantity ten thousand," Ug said, getting right down to business. "I used spot pricing for the nano-gyroscopes, which are a Gem product, but we could probably beat them down on quantity, and I know they need the business. The Verlock has a source for magnetic monopoles, which are a specialty item with them, and we have a group manufacturing cheap superconductors right here…"

"I don't really have any experience with purchasing," Dorothy interrupted. "Shaina and Brinda handle the business stuff on the station, and Jeeves has been dealing with you. What did he say, exactly?"

"My interpretation of the authorization I received from Stryx Jeeves extends sufficient leeway in terms of credit and negotiating power for me to make the deal."

"Are you sure about this, Dorothy?" Kevin asked.

"I am. Just do it, Ug, and send Jeeves the details. What kind of lead time are we talking about?"

"Between setting up the machining and bringing in the materials, I estimate two point seven cycles before the first samples come off the line. But be aware that Drilyenth's algorithms are specific to his wife, and somebody will have to tweak them for every humanoid type. A torque change that indicates a Verlock female losing her balance will be very different from whatever stresses you generate."

"I've never fallen off of heels," Dorothy fibbed, and took a sip from her glass, which she instantly spat out on the Sharf artificial person's chest. "That burns!"

"We wouldn't drink it if it didn't burn—cleanly, I might add," Ug replied. "Fortunately, it also dries without leaving spots." He took the glass that the girl had returned to the tray, and before downing the contents, he spilled a safe amount off into one of the glasses with water to create a weak cocktail for her. "I know that your species has a limited sensor suite, but couldn't you have at least sniffed it first?"

Fifteen

"I hope your rooms were suitable," Kelly said to the Alt leader when she picked up the delegation at the casino/hotel complex just up the corridor from the Empire Convention Center. "I usually try to host visiting diplomats in my home, but you're such a large group."

"The rooms were splendid," Methan replied, though Kelly had an intuition that something wasn't quite right.

"Are you sure there isn't anything else you need? Was the simultaneous translation of the entertainment feeds hard to understand? You don't have to be embarrassed to tell the Stryx about things like that, but I'll be happy to talk to them for you."

"The translations were almost too good," Rinla said, causing her husband to grimace. "Ambassador McAllister said we needn't be embarrassed, and I don't want to think what the children might get into their heads over the course of a few days. Just look how it affected us."

Kelly nodded sympathetically. "I think I understand. I haven't stayed in a hotel for a while, but I imagine that some of the entertainment options they bring in could strike you as offensive. Did you activate the parental monitor? These hotels count on family business, and I'm sure they have a filter that would limit your feed to just the news and shows for children."

"It's the news that was the problem," Methan admitted. "Rinla and I shut it off after just a few minutes, but we had trouble getting those images out of our heads. Then the children came in and said that they had been watching in their own room, and of course, they had nightmares."

"I still don't understand why we had to sleep apart from the children in the first place," his wife said. "That was scary enough for them to start."

"How could we not use both of the rooms when the Stryx insisted on giving us such a beautiful suite?" Methan replied. "It would have been fine if not for that so-called news."

"The Grenouthian broadcasts do tend to focus on, er, strong visuals," Kelly said apologetically. "I hope that at least you had a good breakfast."

"It was almost like home," Rinla replied. "Everything was very similar to what I would serve, though it all tasted just a bit stale."

"I can't even imagine where they came up with the produce and baked goods," Methan added. "I know from our initial reception on the science ship that the other aliens can all eat our fruit without harm, but I'm sure we were told that it doesn't work the other way around."

"It generally doesn't," Kelly agreed, leading the group into the Empire Convention Center. "The Drazens have cast-iron stomachs, and the older a species is, the more likely they can eat cross-cuisine without getting poisoned, but that doesn't mean they enjoy it. My guess is that you were given a synthesized meal, probably based on a chemical analysis of your native food provided by Stryx Wylx."

"The dining room manager said that we were eating off of the Human menu," one of the other Alts volunteered.

"Maybe the species that look similar can eat the same food."

"Not as a rule, though we can eat some of the Vergallian produce," Kelly replied, coming to a halt in front of the entrance to the Nebulae Room. A glimmer of suspicion about the Alt's breakfast crossed her mind, but she shoved it aside for later consideration. "Now I want to warn you before we go in. I've gotten the impression that your culture is very non-confrontational, so some of the sales-men may strike you as a little pushy."

"They're going to hit us and push us?" Meena squeaked, wrapping her arms around her mother's waist.

"No, nothing like that," Kelly backpedalled, cursing the imperfect ear-clip translators that the Alts had brought from their own world. Jeeves had reprogrammed them to work with the tunnel network languages, but their hard-ware lacked the capacity to contextualize language in real-time. "I meant to say that salesmen can be aggressive—I mean, aggravating."

"It's not so different from what we're used to," Methan said. "Our artists and craftsman can get pretty carried away with sharing the fruits of their labor, and it's hard to walk through an exposition without getting loaded down with gifts."

"Just don't sign anything or agree to offer verbal con-firmation if somebody specifically asks you to state your acceptance," the EarthCent ambassador warned them. "If you have questions, just ask me or any of the other ambas-sadors, except maybe the Grenouthian, since he works on commission. Come to think of it, maybe you should stick with asking me."

After the group fanned out into the enormous exposi-tion hall, Kelly trailed along with Methan's family, trying to stay out of the way. The first booth in their path was empty, save for an impressive hologram of a slowly rotating world. As soon as the Alts came to a halt, a giant Dollnick stepped forward and began pointing out salient features of the world with his four hands working at once, all while talking a light-year a minute.

"Some species waste generations exploring the galaxy in search of suitable worlds to colonize, or even just for a vacation home. With our terraforming skill, we can start with a lifeless rock, and in a few short generations you'll have the ideal world, built exactly to your specifications. I understand that your homeworld is the result of terraforming."

"Yes, it is," Methan replied. "We weren't aware that it was so common."

"Done commonly, yes. Done well, no," the Dollnick said. "We have the largest inventory of properly titled planets on the tunnel network so there will never be a question of ownership, and of course we provide Stryx certification that no native life forms are present before we begin. How many can I put you down for?"

"If nothing is living there, why would we want to go?" Meena piped up.

"So you can bring all of your little friends from home. Here, let's zoom in on a simulation we've been working up in anticipation of your arrival. It should be finished by now."

Even though the hologram remained the same size, the surface seemed to rush outward until the blue water and white clouds gave way to rolling fields and vast forests. A small herd of some sort rushed into view, and then the perspective eased into a new angle, showing the world from ground level. Baby deer frolicked around a small girl who was feeding a unicorn something out of her hands. She looked up and smiled out of the hologram, a mirror image of the Alt girl.

"Oh, Daddy, can we get it?" Meena begged. "I'll be so good."

"You're already so good that we wouldn't notice the difference," Methan said with an indulgent smile. "I suppose it wouldn't hurt to learn the price."

A pained look fled across the Dollnick's features. "We're talking about a whole world to design, and a brand new future for billions of people. You can't think of a terraforming project in terms of creds."

"Does that mean it's free?" Meena asked excitedly.

"If you amortize the cost over the generations who will live there, it may as well be free," the salesman agreed with the little girl. "How about it, folks? If we close right now, you'll save enough in legal and realtor fees for an inland ocean—freshwater or salt."

"Please, Daddy," Meena pleaded. "We need somewhere to go in our spaceship."

"It is very nice," Rinla said. "But it wouldn't do to buy the first terraformed world we see without at least looking at the others."

Methan sighed. "I didn't even know we were shopping for a world, but I can take it up with the council of peers when we return home. Thank you for your presentation."

"Prule," the Dollnick identified himself, shoving business chits at the Alts with four hands. "I'm the exclusive representative of Prince Kuerda at this event. If you don't like the financing proposal outlined on this data crystal, you can provide the skilled labor for two other terraforming jobs and we'll barter you a barren planet and lease you the equipment to do the job yourselves."

Kelly couldn't help lingering behind to ask, "How long does all of this take?"

"A couple of generations, unless they're as short-lived as you," Prule replied absent-mindedly before calling after the Alts. "Don't accept cheap imitations from the Drazens or the Frunge. They're still working the bugs out of their terraformed planets, and I mean that literally."

Kelly caught up with the Alt family at the next booth, where a Frunge was enthusiastically demonstrating a bicycle on a treadmill, a shock to the ambassador, who had never seen or heard of a Frunge riding a bike.

"...and the tire treads are specially designed not to create grooves in the soil when you ride off-path, preventing erosion caused by rain runoff," the salesman was saying. "We also have interchangeable seats for both sexes, and the crossbar can be removed for modesty."

"Our manufacturers back home have been trying without success to design erosion-safe tires for years," Rinla admitted. "Can you explain how they work?"

"A wire mesh of smart-metal embedded in the treads continually reshapes the outer surface into random patterns. The photovoltaic cells on the frame which power the process have been doped specifically for your sun, and there's a backup battery integrated in tubing here, and here," the salesman explained, pointing out the power cell locations as he spoke.

Methan looked longingly at the bike, but then he shook his head. "I'm afraid my people haven't fully discussed the whole idea of imports, but I'm sure as soon as we return home it will be at the top of the agenda."

"Here, take this one as a sample." The Frunge hopped off the bicycle, and with a few swift moves, folded it into a package no bigger than a gym bag. Even the wheels and tires folded down without deflating. "If you pull on the green tab, you get the bike, and the brown tab unfolds into a baby stroller."

"What a tremendous advance in technology!" Rinla cried, accepting the package. "And it's so light that a child could carry it."

"I'm not sure we should…" Methan began.

"No obligation, none at all," the Frunge insisted. "Besides, if you force me to take it back, the shame will likely kill me."

"What do you think, Ambassador?" Methan asked Kelly. Behind him, both the salesman and the Alt family were frantically indicating their shared opinion to the ambassador through mime.

"The Frunge do have a culture of gift-giving," Kelly replied slowly. "And he did say no obligation."

"Fine, it's settled then," the Frunge said, breaking into a broad smile. "And watch out for the Dollnick pushing remanufactured space elevators."

"They aren't in good shape?" Methan asked, peering down the aisle at a hologram of a working space elevator that went right up to the ceiling.

"They're just as good as when they were first installed, maybe better. But a space elevator is the single biggest piece of infrastructure on most worlds, so if you're going to splash out for one, you may as well get the latest model," the Frunge offered helpfully.

Rinla hung back with Kelly as her husband and children proceeded to the next booth, where a Horten team was demonstrating a game that involved holograms of barnyard animals. Within two minutes of slipping on the glove controller, Meena mastered the skill of feeding baby

178

chicks with an eyedropper and leveled up to the tricky task of removing porcupine quills from a dog's nose.

"Is this whole exposition really just for us?" Rinla asked quietly. "There must be at least three times as many alien salespeople in here as Alts. I can understand the gentlemen trying to sell us worlds or space elevators, but how can it be worth the time of the plant-like fellow with the bicycle, or this colorful alien demonstrating a game to my daughter?"

"I'm not a business person myself, but I suppose they're all just trying to get a foot in the door," Kelly explained. "When my people joined the tunnel network, we didn't have anything of value to offer the aliens, other than our labor. They didn't start seeing us as a market for goods until around twenty years ago, and they're still cautious about extending credit to Earth because we're only probationary members of the tunnel network."

"We've only just developed faster-than-light drive ourselves, and some of us worry that a flood of alien imports would ruin our native industries. Did the availability of alien goods and technology short-circuit your own economy?"

"Our economy was already on the rocks when the Stryx stepped in, and then more than half of our population left Earth, mainly on alien labor contracts. Our diplomatic service has been working hard to attract alien businesses, and humans are now manufacturing some advanced technology under license, but I guess you could say there was a pretty big disruption."

"Did the other species open their education system to Humans?"

"The best universities in the galaxy are the ones run by the Stryx, and they're open to everybody. But the aliens are all pretty traditional, so they mainly prefer going through their own systems, which tend to be highly specialized according to the cultural priorities of each species."

"What about your own family?" the Alt pressed Kelly. "I'd like to know what choices you made."

"Our children attended the Open University, and my son is currently taking courses there. My brother's family is still on Earth, and his grandchildren are attending a magnet school that's managed by the Verlocks in their academy style. I think my grandniece is going to a Vergallian dance academy on Earth as well."

"Look what Mr. Norna gave me," Meena said, waving her gloved hand and a small hologame cube. "It's so different from our games. I can barter my completed chores to pay for veterinary services for the animals, or in an emergency, he said I can use currency." She turned to Kelly and asked, "What's a programmable cred?"

"A Stryx currency holder accepted by all of the tunnel network species. It's real money, not a game thing, though I suppose selling points to children is better than usury."

"I didn't understand a word you used. You-something?"

"Usury is lending money at an unreasonably high rate of interest. Like, I'll give you five coins today, but tomorrow you have to pay me back six."

"Our translation devices were designed for understanding dolphins and dogs," Methan explained. "Dolphins have no use for money and dogs can't hold onto it, so it's not surprising that our hardware lacks the capacity for dealing with financial concepts that are absent from our own economy."

"You could let the Stryx provide you with their translation earpieces," Kelly suggested. "You don't have to accept implants if you don't want them."

"A little filtering can be a good thing," the Alt replied, and then crouched to talk to his daughter. "We planned on explaining alien concepts of money when you were a bit older, but think of it as a substitute for keeping track of the time people spend doing useful work."

"Why?" Meena asked. "It's easy for everybody to carry a block to keep track of the time they spend contributing to the community." She dug in her handbag and came up with a small tan slab of a plastic-like substance with a stylus clipped to the side.

"But the alien species needed a universal medium of exchange," Methan said, drawing a blank look from his daughter. "I hate to…" he looked up at his wife, who gave him a sad nod. "It's that some people use their imaginations about how much time they've worked, or how useful that work is."

"Imagination? Like in the story we told on 'Let's Make Friends?'"

"Yes, but instead of telling stories about space monsters, they tell stories about jobs they've performed when they haven't."

A tragic look settled on the little girl's features as the meaning sank in, and she asked in a shaky voice, "But if they make up numbers on their blocks, how can I trust them?"

"We'll talk more about this when we get home," her father said gently. "Just remember that your family loves you and we'll always be there if you need us."

"I think his highness is waking up," Rinla said, looking down at the tiny face in her baby sling. "Why don't you carry Meena's things, Methan, and she can hold him for me."

The family reshuffled their burdens, and the girl regained her composure as soon as the baby was in her arms. Then they moved on as a group to the next booth, where a baby boy similar to Meena's charge was the only item on offer. Then Chastity popped up from behind the counter, a stack of disposable tabs in her hands.

"Great, I got here in time," the publisher of the Galactic Free Press said. "Oh, what a lovely baby, he looks around the same age as mine. Are you the mommy?" she teased the little girl.

"I believe you already met on Stryx Wylx's science ship," Kelly said, but added a reminder for the Alts, "This is Chastity Papamarkakis, who runs the main human newspaper, among other things."

"Wow, what a great name," a breathless boy exclaimed.

"Antha! Where have you been since breakfast?" his mother admonished him.

"Out and about," the boy said evasively. "Mr. Jeeves was showing me the station. I wanted to see the Drazen deck."

"There's a story about it right here," Chastity said, distributing tabs to the surprised Alts.

Meena didn't have a free hand due to holding the baby, but she looked at the tab that Chastity held up for her. "You publish your newspaper in Alt?"

"It's a new version, as of this morning. We're looking to hire an Alt editor if you know anybody who would be interested. I'm sure Libby got the translation and grammar correct, but she's kind of expensive."

"Alt boy signs treaty with Drazens," Methan read the headline.

Kelly stared at the picture, which showed Antha and the Drazen ambassador holding up a document together. "I can't believe Bork would do something like this, or that Jeeves would go along with it. It's a good thing your son is just a child or it could be legally binding."

"Don't the Drazens recognize children's rights?" Rinla asked indignantly.

"They do, actually, but I thought your species might have a legal age for signing contracts. You don't?"

"It hasn't come up before," Methan said with a frown. "Do you remember what this document said, Antha?"

"Sure. Uncle Bork asked the station librarian to read it for me. It said that we're friends and that if I ever know somebody making a moving picture story who needs an actor with a tentacle, I'm supposed to contact the Drazen embassy on Union Station."

"That's very kind of him. It would be difficult for one of our own people to play a Drazen convincingly. I hope you thanked Mr. Jeeves and Uncle Bork."

"I forgot," the boy cried, and raced off before his parents could stop him.

"This is a nice story," Meena said, having moved past the picture and caption. "It's about children who baked cookies and bartered them for paint to make their playhouse pretty."

"In the Galactic Free Press?" Kelly looked over the girl's shoulder, but the Alt text was all gibberish to her.

"I gave them the syndicated feed from the teacher bot student newspapers we're picking up," Chastity explained. "From what the Grenouthians tell me, I think the Alts may want to stick with watching the Children's News Network until they get the hang of the galaxy."

"Is this free?" Meena asked cautiously.

"One hundred percent. And once we figure out what you're interested in, you'll even get special content from our sponsors at no extra charge."

Sixteen

"Did it bother you that I was still spending all of that time in dance practice with Samuel after you began working for InstaSitter this year?" Vivian asked her brother.

"Are you kidding? Libby started paying me five creds an hour after I completed my training."

"Don't you mean InstaSitter started paying you?"

"She does the payroll, you know. Anyway, Tinka calls this the 'War Room,' because Libby routes us all of the emergency pings that come up," Jonah explained.

"But I don't know anything about medical stuff, and I can't believe you would give advice to babysitters with a sick alien kid!"

"Boy, you really have been out of the loop, haven't you?" her brother said sympathetically. "Libby handles all of the sick calls by having Gryph send a medbot. We just get the parental emergencies and the occasional panic call from a sitter."

"Parental emergencies? Like they don't want to go home to their kids?"

"Don't laugh. We've had people abandon children with the sitter, though they're usually not the biological parents, but Libby handles those as well."

"Does she stop them from leaving the station?"

"You know how the Stryx are about stuff like that. Libby figures that anybody who runs out on a child isn't the best caretaker option, so she has the sitter bring the kid to the station orphanage while she checks for other relatives."

"Does it happen often?"

"We've got over twenty million sitters of all species working on Stryx stations," Jonah reminded her. "Sometimes a single parent leaves their kids with a sitter and dies of natural causes while out dancing or playing sports. One way or another, it happens every day."

"I'm glad we don't get those pings, then. But what are we doing here?"

"I'm getting to it," her brother said, clearly enjoying himself. "First, can you show her the active roster, Libby?"

A list of names began scrolling down the large screen in front of the siblings, moving so fast that the lines of text were little more than a black blur. Several other columns of information appeared after the names, but Vivian also noticed that little colored comets were shooting by on the left side of the screen.

"Could you pause on a red dot?" Jonah requested.

The list came to a sudden halt, though despite being stationary, most of the phonetically spelled alien names in the first column still made for difficult reading. There was a large red dot to the left of the name in the center of the display field, but the columns relating to billing status, species, working conditions, and on-time returns all looked normal.

"Dollnicks," Vivian read from the species column. "So why do Kunda and Shuerna get the red star?"

"Libby? Can you play back their last call sequence, with security imaging?"

The screen changed from the text list to showing a teenage Drazen girl sitting on the edge of a large nest. She was watching some sort of drama on a tab held in one hand, while her other hand dangled in the nest, where it was clutched by a sleeping Dollnick baby.

"Everything looks fine to me," Vivian commented.

Jonah just grinned and pointed at the screen. A little message appeared in the upper left corner, reading, "Incoming ping from Kunda."

A long-suffering look appeared on the young Drazen's face, but she accepted the ping, and said, "InstaSitter Minka here. He's still breathing, Kunda."

"Are you sure?" a nervous voice asked. "Have you checked his body temperature?"

"He's holding my hand," the sitter replied patiently. "I scanned his vitals for you five minutes ago."

"Minka? This is Shuerna. Couldn't you check again, and run the full scan this time?"

The Drazen girl rolled her eyes, but reached up to a shelf beside the nest with her tentacle and retrieved a baby health monitor, which looked like a cross between a tab and a ray gun. She pointed it at the baby, and then brought it around so she could see the display.

"Everything looks the same as five minutes ago," she reported dutifully.

"What about his brain waves?" Shuerna asked anxiously. "My great-grandsire suffered from abnormal patterns."

"As a baby?" Minka inquired.

"No, he was in his six-hundreds, but it's hereditary."

"The brain waves look perfect," the sitter responded, without bothering to change screens. "Is there anything else?"

"No. Thank you so much. We'll ping back during intermission."

The Drazen girl shook her head and returned the baby monitor to its shelf. She smiled at the sleeping Dollnick infant, who really was cute in his four-armed romper suit, and then went back to watching the drama on her tab. The time stamp on the image jumped forward five minutes, and a message appeared in the upper left corner, reading, "Incoming ping from Kunda."

"InstaSitter Minka," the Drazen girl answered.

"I'm so sorry to bother you, but I forgot to ask if you checked his temperature."

"Actually, you did, and it's still normal," the girl responded, without even looking up from her drama.

"Minka? This is Shuerna. If it's not too much trouble, can you tell if his eyes are moving beneath the lids? I know that Drazens don't have the same depth perception that we do, but..."

"Yes, he's dreaming up a storm. If his eyes were moving any faster I'd be worried that it was a nightmare."

"Do you really think it's a bad dream? We could come home early."

"No, it's just a Drazen saying about healthy eye movements," the girl replied. "Was there anything else?"

"Sorry for bothering you. You're our favorite sitter, you know."

"Thank you, Libby," Jonah said, and the screen reverted to showing the scrolling list of names. "It usually goes on like that all evening with the red dotters. The sitters get hazard pay."

"That's really sad, but where do we come in?"

"Sometimes the sitters run out of patience and say something snarky, and then the parents ask to speak to a supervisor."

"Oh. What were the other color codes?"

"Can we see an orange dot, Libby?"

"There's a code orange coming in right now," the station librarian replied, and the screen zoomed in on a text line with an orange dot to the left of the names.

"Pyun Woojin?" Vivian read in disbelief.

"Mr. Pyun?" Jonah spoke in no particular direction.

"Jonah? Is that you?"

"Yes, Mr. Pyun. How can we help you today?"

"I'm a little uncomfortable with the sitter you sent out. I know it was a last minute thing, but Thomas and Chance are also attending the banquet for the Alts, so we were stuck."

"What exactly worries you about Bortu?"

"We've never had a Horten boy sit for Em before. In my experience, young Horten males aren't that responsible."

"It's true that most of our Horten sitters are girls, but the boys who pass InstaSitter screening are equally quali-fied, and Bortu has completed over fifty assignments without a complaint. Besides, you know that Libby is always watching."

"The bag he was carrying looked like it might have con-tained a…"

"Are you pestering InstaSitter again?" Lynx's voice broke into the discussion. "I can't leave you alone for a minute to go to the bathroom. I'm beginning to think that you're the one who needs babysitting."

"It's just that the Horten boy might have a game console with him. You know how immersive those things are."

"InstaSitter bans game consoles during work," Jonah reminded Woojin.

"Is that you, Jonah?" Lynx asked.

"Yes, Mrs. Pyun."

"Don't call me that. It's plain 'Lynx.' Can I get a sitter for my husband?"

"Can't a father show concern for his daughter without being treated like there's something wrong with him?" Woojin demanded.

"There is something wrong with you," Lynx retorted. "I thought that marrying an ex-mercenary with over twenty years of combat experience would spare me from this kind of discussion."

"Thank you for pinging InstaSitter," Jonah said, and made a slicing motion under his throat. Then he grinned at his twin, and they both dissolved in laughter.

"So orange is for parents who complain about the sitters?" Vivian asked when she recovered.

"Specifically the parents who worry that every new sitter isn't appropriate. Libby tries to schedule the same sitter for them whenever possible, but the Pyuns usually get free babysitting from Thomas or Chance, so there aren't that many candidates."

"What about the other colors."

"Can we see a gold dot, Libby?"

"Gold sounds good," Vivian said, watching as the screen changed to display a new set of names. "Wait a minute. Isn't Abeva the Vergallian Ambassador?"

"Yes. The daughters of the Vergallian upper caste can get pretty out of control when they're children. It's like some of them have a genetic predisposition to command, so you can't tell them anything."

"And that earns the mother a gold star?"

"Her daughter, Aciva, is in our top one-tenth of one percent. That's what the gold star means."

"What is she at the top for? Bad behavior?"

"Babysitting hours. Abeva works all the time, and she left her husband or whoever behind when she took the assignment on Union Station. Mom said that normally the embassy staff would be stuck taking care of the ambassador's daughter, but I guess it caused a lot of problems, because Abeva hires InstaSitters every day. We used to have somebody there basically around the clock, but Aciva turned four last cycle, which means she has tutors for part of the day now. Sitting for her was kind of a blast."

"You've babysat the Vergallian ambassador's daughter?"

"Sure. You're going to have to get your hours in too, you know. Mom's a big believer in nepotism, but you still have to learn the ropes."

"What was she like?"

"Aciva? Most beautiful little girl you ever saw until I refused to let her play with the kitchen knives. First, she held her breath until she fainted, which freaked me out pretty good. Then when she came to, she bit my thumb. I still have a scar. See?"

"What did you do then?"

"I let her play with the kitchen knives." Jonah watched his twin's eyes go wide, and broke into another grin. "Just kidding. I washed it off and then I chased her around the apartment until she was tired enough to go to sleep."

"What did Abeva say when she came home?"

"She tipped me fifty creds! I loved sitting for Aciva after that."

"Panic call," the station librarian reported. This time, a different text grid appeared on the screen, one that showed the names of sitters and their track records. Vivian immediately saw that the highlighted name, Dianne Farnsworth, was on just her fourth assignment, and the first one sitting for an alien child.

"Dianne," Jonah said in a voice that sounded much more mature than his fourteen years. "What seems to be the problem?"

"Missra has disappeared!"

"I'm sure she's still in the apartment or our security monitor would have informed you," Jonah said, and mouthed 'Libby,' at his sister. "She's probably playing hide-and-seek."

"I know she's playing hide-and-seek, but I was looking right at her and she suddenly vanished."

"I see this is your first time babysitting for a Chert. Did she have a device mounted on her shoulder?"

"Yes. She made me wait to start the game while she put it on. I thought it was some kind of camera."

"No, it's an invisibility projector. Do you have a tab with you?"

"Yes, I was going to do my homework later."

"Turn it on and I'll request the station librarian to render the 3D security imaging into a flat screen feed for you. Chert technology can't fool the Stryx."

"You're a life saver," Dianne said. A moment later, the twins heard her yelling into her InstaSitter-provided external translator, "Missra! Your mom said no snacks before bedtime. The kitchen is officially out of bounds now."

"You're really good at this," Vivian complimented her brother.

"You'll get the hang of it. Tinka says that babysitting is in our blood."

"Does she still get all whacky every time her family forces her out on an arranged date?"

"Did you notice the flowers on the receptionist's desk when you came in?"

"What about them?"

"We have an early warning system. When Tinka has an arranged date, Aunt Chas stops in and adds a black rose to the arrangement. You can't miss it."

"I have so much to catch up on. I mean, I wouldn't trade my seven years of dance practice with Samuel for anything, but with mom insisting that we sleep nine hours a night, there just wasn't enough time for everything."

"What are you going to do if he goes away to be with Ailia when he finishes school?" Jonah asked suddenly. "You saw them at Dring's ball."

"That's when I lost interest in Vergallian dancing," Vivian admitted. "I could never be as graceful as her. It's also when I realized that he must have some secret way for them to practice together, because no couple could have danced like that their first time."

"That's impossible."

"When I asked Sam about the dance steps he added to our routines, he always said he learned them from Vergallian dramas, but I know that they were new. And I noticed that he has everything in his room pushed up against the walls, like he needs the floor space for dancing. I think Jeeves fixed them up with some way of visiting each other in real-time, like holograms or something."

"You've been in his bedroom? I thought he didn't let anybody except for Beowulf in there."

"Since I started fencing with him he lets me keep my stuff in his closet. He's really good with a sword. I have to cheat like crazy to beat him."

"It's like you're betting all your chips on him staying," Jonah cautioned her.

"He's going to marry me," Vivian stated flatly.

"You don't think it's a little weird to be that set on who you're going to marry at our age? I don't think about that stuff at all."

"That's because you're a boy. Girls have to be smart about these things."

"You're always saying stuff like that," her brother complained.

"It's true, though. One of my courses in Dynastic Studies …"

"Code Blue," Libby interrupted, and the operations screen popped up the relevant assignment parameters.

"InstaSitter Central. How can I help you?" Jonah said immediately.

Vivian wondered why he hadn't used the client's name since the text was right there on the screen, but then she read the species entry and saw that the parents were Grenouthian.

"I just came home and found that your sitter had completely ignored my instructions, and on top of that, she was very rude to me," a voice complained.

"I'm sure it was just a cultural misunderstanding," the boy replied. "We train our Verlock sitters to speak very bluntly in order to save time."

"She told ME to calm down!"

"Could I ask what instructions she failed to carry out?"

"I specifically told her that my children are prohibited from watching Vergallian dramas. But when I came home, the holo was playing action highlights from…"

"Panic call," Libby cut into the audio stream. "It's the Verlock sitter."

Jonah glanced at the new data on the screen and said, "Glythianor. Your client is currently making a complaint."

"Her eyes are all bugged out and she stopped yelling at me," the excited Verlock girl said at an almost normal clip. "I thought she was having a stroke."

"No, she's just subvocing us and getting worked up. I'll ping you back. Libby?"

"You haven't missed anything," the station librarian commented. "Switching back."

"...situations inappropriate for their age. And furthermore, I resent the implication that it's my fault for not specifying that Grenouthian documentaries about Vergallian dramas were also banned."

"I understand," Jonah said, making a circular motion near the side of his head with his forefinger. "You're home now, and even the Stryx can't reverse time, so I'll take Glythianor off the list of sitter candidates for your address. Will that be satisfactory?"

"I think an apology is in order."

"I'm very sorry for your inconvenience."

"I meant from the sitter!"

"I'm very sorry, but I'm just a human so I can't request that from a member of an advanced species," Jonah said. The bunny sniffed loudly and disconnected.

"Just a human?" Vivian said, her face reddening.

"I pull that one out at least once a shift. We have a manual on using self-deprecating humor to defuse tense situations, but I'm too stupid to remember where I put it."

"Don't ever say that about yourself. I'm just sensitive because of what I had to put up with from the aliens when I started in Dynastic Studies, and—you just used it on me, didn't you."

"Yup. Libby got Jeeves to write it for us. He's a customer service genius."

"Since when?"

"He used to handle all of the problem cases for Libby's dating service. Some of those messy dates make babysitter complaints look like a minor irritation."

"How would you know?"

"Libby lets me answer some of them when things are slow with InstaSitter. Just the human singles."

"Seriously, though. Why doesn't she handle all of the InstaSitter complaints without us? You know she'd be better at it."

"Tinka said it's less expensive this way."

"But Libby is the one setting the price, and she can charge whatever she wants. Oh, I get it."

"Besides, it's good training for management. Tinka runs all of the promising hires through the war room to see how they handle the pressure. Want to try the next one?"

"Sure," Vivian said, though she began twisting a strand of hair around her finger, a sure sign of nerves. "Libby? How come you don't just show nervous parents the station security imaging when they call in?"

"That would be an invasion of privacy," the station librarian replied.

"But you're always watching anyway."

"I'm very discrete so it doesn't count."

"Are you implying that biologicals can't keep a secret?" Vivian demanded.

"Compared to me, you're a cipher," Jonah answered for the station librarian. He added in a dejected tone, "Mom says that I could never be a spy because I'm too talkative."

"That's not true. Spies need to be good communicators, and you talk less than—you're using that stupid manual on me again. Aren't you?"

Jonah brushed an imaginary speck of dust off his shoulder. "We've got a copy at home you can read. Jeeves also licensed it to EarthCent Intelligence."

Seventeen

Have you ever been to a Vergallian world before?" Dorothy asked Kevin.

"Not to land," he told her. "The whole tech-ban thing gets on my nerves, and the queens are basically absolute rulers in their domains. I've heard rumors about traders setting down and never getting permission to leave again, though there are stories like that about most places. The only reason I agreed to this stop is that we have your friend's guarantee."

"She's really my brother's friend. I didn't even get a chance to talk to her when she came back to Union Station for the ball that Dring threw for my mom." Dorothy twisted around to look at the dog curled up in his basket. "So when are you going to wake Alexander from his Zero-G hibernation?"

"I already did. He's sleeping now because he likes to sleep. Maybe he knew we'd end up sitting on the ground for hours waiting on her royal highness."

"I'm sure there's a reason. She's not the type to play status games with people. They probably don't get many spaceships landing here so they aren't prepared."

"That guy on the ground control circuit sounded pretty out of it," Kevin admitted. "Who did he say he'd notify?"

"The stable master. At least he didn't ask you to hand over control of the ship."

"He was pretty firm about our remaining onboard until somebody comes for us, though. Hey, are we in the path of a cavalry charge?"

Dorothy ran to press her nose against the port while Kevin brought up an external image of the approaching riders on the main screen. The horses were thundering across the tarmac at a full gallop, their riders maintaining a tight military formation.

"I think that's Ailia in the middle, next to the guy with the banner. And those look like Earth horses."

"Horses mean that they must be a human mercenary detachment," Kevin observed, "And they all have banners."

"But only one of them is riding next to Ailia," Dorothy said, completing the circle of her logic.

"I doubt they've got any equipment to ping us up here so we better go drop the ramp." Kevin went over and roused the dog. "Into the dumbwaiter, boy. You can't take the ladder while we're on a planet. It's straight down."

Alexander didn't even bother stretching when he rose. Instead he trotted over to the box-like cable elevator Joe had rigged so the dog could access both the bridge and the technical deck under gravity conditions. The Cayl hound curled up in the box and took his tail in his mouth to make sure it didn't get caught between decks.

"Beat you down," Kevin challenged Alexander, punching the button for the pulley motor and then racing for the ladder. Unfortunately, Dorothy had gotten there before him, and she wasn't about to try a fireman's slide for the sake of a bet with the dog, who always won anyway.

"Pretty clever of my dad to think of a dog elevator," Dorothy said as she clambered down the long ladder. "I don't remember there being one on the Nova."

"Beowulf usually goes down to the technical deck by himself when we're returning to Union Station, though I remember one time that everybody forgot. We had to rig up a harness, and then the three of us helped him rappel down the ladder."

"That couldn't have been easy. I bet he weighs more than dad."

"He took a lot of his own weight on his paws, though I don't think he enjoyed being pulled from two directions at once. Joe swore that Beowulf can take a vertical ladder by himself if there's food at the top, but going down backwards is asking a lot, even from a Cayl hound."

Alexander was already out of the dumbwaiter and waiting when Kevin and Dorothy reached the deck. He knew better than to rush to the cargo container hatch, where his lack of thumbs put him at a distinct disadvantage versus the humans. Instead, he hung back doing doggy yoga and trying to look bored.

"Will Alex be able to make it down the stairs you guys welded to the side of the container?"

"Sure. Sometimes back at Mac's Bones he'd run up and down them while I was working, just to irritate me."

As soon as the hatch was open, Alexander proved the truth of Kevin's words by slipping past the people and barreling down the stairs so fast that Dorothy was sure he would crash into something at the bottom. But the dog turned and raced for the container's main hatch, where he stood on his hind legs and held his paw just a hair above the ramp button.

"Wait," Kevin commanded in a stern voice. "If the Vergallians see you standing there by yourself, they'll assume that you ate us, and then where will you be?"

"Now he's going to start thinking about food," Dorothy said. "When's the last time he did eat?"

"I'm not sure, but I'm also not worried about it. If I know one thing about dogs, it's that they'll find a way to let you know when they're hungry."

After they reached the bottom of the stairs and started for the main hatch, Dorothy asked, "How do you know if there's even space to lower the ramp when there aren't any viewports down here?"

"Ship," Kevin called out. "Is there room to lower the ramp?"

"Affirmative," the controller replied.

"Go ahead, Alex."

The dog depressed the button with his paw and the main hatch slowly folded outwards, transforming into a ramp hinged at the deck. Kevin stood in the center of the opening, keeping both of his hands in plain sight, and warned the dog against racing out before they had permission.

The ramp wasn't halfway down before Alexander scrambled out and ran into the shadows under the ship.

"Where do you think he's—oh, I get it," Dorothy said.

When the ramp touched the tarmac, the dog came trotting back up, acting like nothing had happened. A few seconds later the riders rounded the blast wall on the landing pad and trotted towards the ship. As the troop came to a halt a short distance from the ramp, a number of hounds which had been running alongside the horses sniffed at the air and then dashed under the ship to investigate. Alexander gave his humans an enormous tongue-lolling grin.

"Dorothy McAllister?" the official herald cried in a loud voice.

"Here," Dorothy replied, half raising her hand.

"Welcome to our domains in the name of Royal Protector Baylit, acting in the interest of Ailia, heir to the throne of Avidiya, daughter of Atuba, granddaughter of Avilia, great-granddaughter of Aagra. You are granted tarmac space in the restricted zone for your ship, though any goods you bring into the realm are subject to our rules regarding technology. Baylit offers you hearth and home for as long as you choose to remain."

"Uh, thank you very much," Dorothy replied, unsure if a formulaic response was required. "Can we come out now?"

"Yes, the ceremony is over," Ailia called, pushing past the large horse on which the herald was mounted. "That's as short as I could get him to make it. Can you ride?"

"How well trained are those things?" Kevin asked.

"You'd have to work to fall off of the ones we brought for you," the Vergallian girl told him with a grin. "I don't imagine Dorothy gets a lot of riding opportunities on Union Station."

"Like zero," Dorothy confirmed, coming down the ramp and dropping a polite curtsey. Kevin fumbled his way through an awkward bow.

"Is that Beowulf?" Ailia asked in surprise, approaching the giant dog. "He hasn't aged a day, though he seems smaller than my memory. It must be because I was so little."

"This is Alexander," Kevin explained. "Beowulf's son."

The Vergallian dogs returned from their visit under the ship to investigate the perpetrator, and a bout of intense sniffing took place on all sides. Then a small rodent scolded them from its perch on the low blast wall, and all of the dogs took off as one in its direction.

"They're palace dogs," Ailia explained apologetically. "Real cavalry dogs would have more discipline. I rushed over as soon as the stable master brought the news of your arrival, but communications between the port and the stables are by runner."

"Let me grab your presents and close up the ship," Kevin said. It only took him a minute to reappear with a large pack, after which he instructed the ship to raise the hatch.

Ailia swung herself gracefully into the saddle, and attendants helped Dorothy and Kevin mount their rides. Then the herald sounded a note on a small horn, and the horses broke into a canter that felt smoother than it sounded.

"How can you hear each other over this racket?" Dorothy yelled at Ailia.

"What?" the Vergallian princess shouted in response.

"Never mind."

Alexander caught up with the riders before any of the native dogs, looking particularly smug as he bounded alongside Kevin's mount. From the tarmac of the ancient, underutilized spaceport they continued onto a road that wound through endless fields separated by stone walls that fit into the landscape so harmoniously that the scene would have looked unnatural without them. By the time the horses slowed for the palace gates, the sun was beginning to set, and bright lanterns above the streets were being lit by men with long poles.

"Kind of medieval," Dorothy commented to Kevin as he helped her dismount.

"Reminds me of New Kasil. How's your backside?"

"My backside is none of your business. Do you ride often, Princess Ailia?"

"Every day before breakfast," the girl replied with a sigh. "There are twelve roads leading out from the palace, one for each day of the week. If I failed to show myself on one of those roads for two weeks in a row, the nobles of the section would start fighting over my replacement."

"Just like in the dramas," Dorothy said, trying to keep the pity out of her voice. "Do you ever get used to it?"

"Years ago. Come, you must be hungry after waiting at the spaceport and your long ride. I have somewhere special to take you."

"Is it Human Burger?"

"I'm afraid I don't know what that is," the princess replied.

"What a relief. You don't know how that place has haunted our trip."

"I've never set down on a Vergallian world before," Kevin said. "Is there somebody at the spaceport who will approve my goods before I arrange for transport to the closest marketplace?"

"The crown purchases all alien goods arriving at the spaceport," Ailia replied, leading the way through a maze-like series of passages. Four of the guards who had been on the spaceport trip accompanied them silently. "It's the only way to control technology leakage, and exotic imports give us a way of raising revenue from the wealthy."

"My father taught me never to argue with royalty," Kevin said, eyeing the four guards who had stayed within easy reach of Ailia ever since she dismounted.

"A wise man." The princess stopped at a heavy wooden door decorated with a crudely painted stack of gold coins. One of the guards stepped forward and knocked on the heavy strike-plate with his pole-axe. A metal shutter on a small window overlooking the alley swung open, and a head popped out to survey the visitors. There was the muffled sound of a bell ringing, and the door yawned open.

"Welcome to the Mercenary Tavern, Your Highness," a human woman greeted them in English. "We haven't seen you in some time."

"These two are friends of mine," Ailia said. "They are not to be charged if they return without me during their stay at the palace."

"Of course, Your Highness. The private room will be ready in just a moment." The hostess glanced over her shoulder to where tavern staff were hustling a couple of irate mercenaries out of a doorway and into the main room. She nodded with approval. "Please follow me."

"My sister brings me here to meet with the officers of our hired soldiers as part of my training," the princess explained to her guests. "It's traditional for royal families to employ mercenaries in their personal guard, and I try to get Humans whenever possible."

"I remember you couldn't eat chocolate or any of our dairy products," Dorothy said. "Do they serve real human food here, or is it human style?"

"You can eat anything here. Some of it is imported from off-world, some of it is grown in a special allotment we give the men and their families for raising food. They've had very good luck with chickens, which can digest our grains and insects."

The hostess seated the three diners around a heavy wooden table in the small room, but the guards remained standing, two in the hallway and two just inside the door. "Today's special is fried chicken with potatoes and boiled Vergallian greens," she informed them. "I can bring menus if you like, but we had a busy day so we're out of a lot of things."

"Chicken is great," Kevin said. "And if you've got something for the dog."

"We have dog food," the hostess suggested.

Alexander groaned and shook his massive head.

"Some deboned chicken and potatoes would be good. He doesn't care for green vegetables."

"The special for me," Dorothy added. "Are you eating, Ailia?"

"I'll have the same, but substitute a double serving of greens for the chicken," the princess said. "And bring an extra table for the guards to eat in the hall. There's no other way in here, Sven, and we have the dog for backup," she added in the direction of guards.

The taller of the two men who had positioned himself inside the door inclined his head, scowled at Alexander, and withdrew with his fellow guard.

"Now tell me about your family," Ailia continued. "How is Aisha's new baby?"

"Cute, you know what babies are like. And Fenna is growing like a weed. Did you know about Aisha buying Paul a whole fleet of abandoned ships? That's where Kevin got ours from."

"You two got married? Congratulations. I can't believe Samuel didn't tell me."

"We're just traveling together," Dorothy rushed to correct her. "It's Kevin's ship, but after living on it for—wow, is it already a month?"

"We spent a week on the Frunge world, if you include the elevator time, and five days on the Drazen space station. We slept on the ship at Chintoo."

"And you haven't made a formal commitment to each other?" the young princess asked, obviously puzzled.

"We have a Frunge thing," Dorothy explained. "My friend made us get it. I hope you don't need to see it because we left it on the ship."

"No, I brought it in the pack, just in case," Kevin said. "Most of this stuff is gifts for you, Princess, including a bundle from Jeeves."

"I'd like to see the contract if you don't mind. I've been studying jurisprudence, and my tutor pushed me to learn something about the Frunge legal system, since it's the closest to our own."

"You can read Frunge?" Dorothy asked, as Kevin rummaged through his large pack and extracted the inscribed slab.

"Languages are easy for me, probably because I was exposed to a number of them at a young age when I was living on Union Station. Let's see." She started to lift the tablet that Kevin slid across the table and then settled for reading it where it lay. "This all looks like the standard boilerplate, though a number of clauses related to Frunge biology have been omitted. I think it's nice that the terms leave you free to conduct a romance. Everything in Vergallian companionship contracts is about the bottom line."

"I wasn't going to let them put in the number of times a week we, uh…" Dorothy trailed off, remembering that Ailia was younger than she looked.

"I understand perfectly. As long as you do plan to get married in the end."

"I want to marry Kevin. I just don't want to be pushed."

"And I want to marry Dorothy."

"That's settled then," the princess said brightly. "Now tell me about Samuel."

"He works twice as hard as I did when I was his age," Dorothy admitted. "When he's not taking courses at the Open University or practicing ballroom dancing with Vivian, he's working with my dad and Paul, or at the lost-and-found."

"But he gave up competing after you left Union Station," Ailia informed them.

"I forgot you had a secret link with him, so your news is more recent than ours," Dorothy said.

"You knew about that?"

"Come on, he's my little brother. Do you think I'd let him hide something like that from me? I've known for years, but I didn't tell anybody."

"He mentioned that he's fencing with Vivian now, and between the Open University and her visiting him at work, they spend as much time together as ever."

"They're pretty much best friends, and I guess she's got plans," Dorothy said. "You know that her mother was going to marry Paul, but she didn't move fast enough and Aisha came along."

"They all seemed very happy with their choices when I knew them," the princess said. "Do you think Vivian would be good for him?"

"Just because she has plans doesn't mean that he'll go along with them," Dorothy said, misunderstanding Ailia's sad look. "It's not that easy to drag a McAllister to the altar, well, except for my parents of course, and that's just because Libby got involved."

"I'd like you to bring Vivian a gift from me when you go back, but it will take a few days to prepare," Ailia told them. "Don't run off without telling me."

Eighteen

"So we put on these suits and then we can fly?"

"It's more like swimming in air," Paul explained to the leader of the Alt mission. "The levitation suits are calibrated to give you neutral buoyancy, but you can get thrust from the booties for accelerating."

"How can there possibly be rocket engines in these flimsy things?" Methan asked, examining the soles of the shoe covers. "They don't even look like they'd stand up to a strong rain."

"It's just a logical fiction for the humanoids who make up most of the players. You curl your toes to speed up, and the levitation controller actually pulls all of the monopoles woven into your suit forward along the axis of your legs. Most people feel like it's thrust coming from their feet."

"The computational power needed to run this game must require a Stryx!"

"Only for the initial setup," Paul said. "Jeeves repurposed an old Verlock weather control system for the job. I'm sure you know how much math it takes just to predict the weather, so imagine what's required to control it."

"Why would you want to control the weather?" Methan's daughter asked. "It's all part of nature."

"Our world isn't natural, it was made by the Stryx," her younger brother pointed out. "Even I knew that before the aliens came, except for the Stryx part, I mean."

"Those large murals are lovely," Rinla said, hoping to head off an unseemly disagreement between her two oldest children. "We would call it 'Early modern abstract primitive' back home."

"Uh, it's just random paintball splatter," Paul told her. "Back when I was sort of managing the place, I had the maintenance bots clean the walls once a day, but the Dollnick who took over the contract decided it was a waste of creds."

"What do balls of paint have to do with flying?" Methan asked.

"It's part of the game. You have to avoid getting hit while you shoot the other players."

"Shoot? As in, with a … weapon?"

"No, it's just a basket with a small propulsion system built into the handle. Kids love it."

"I'm not so sure about this," Methan said, but Antha and Meena had already pulled on their flying suits and were headed for the lift-off area.

"Go ahead, Methan," Rinla encouraged him. "One of us should keep an eye on the children, and I have to feed Methanon. I'll be right here waiting."

Paul helped the reluctant Alt don the flying suit and escorted him into the game area just as the calliope started wailing.

"Astounding!" Methan declared. "We have an antique pipe organ at our local fairground which is just as badly out of tune."

"Watch your feet," Paul cautioned him from below as the players all rose into the air. "You can move forward using swimming strokes, but remember to activate the booties if you want to go faster. Don't worry about running into anybody. The controller bases your trajectory after an impact on a perfect inelastic collision, but it stretches the time scale to keep the rate of change in your comfort range."

Even as Paul spoke, Antha barreled towards his father at full speed, but at the last moment his vector changed sharply, and Methan's suit suddenly accelerated him off on a tangent at perhaps a quarter of his son's velocity.

"I see why you call it the 'Physics Ride,'" the Alt scientist shouted back at Paul, who waved and walked off of the game floor.

Twenty minutes later, Kelly arrived out of breath and demanded, "Where is he?"

"Lying down behind the rental counter," Paul told her. Between the calliope music and the howling Alt baby he was holding for Rinla, communications were suboptimal. He pointed at two small figures in the corner of the flying space and added, "I promised their parents I'd keep an eye on the kids during the elimination match."

The ambassador glanced in the direction Paul was pointing and was surprised to see two small figures in flying suits floating back to back, shooting a steady stream of paintballs at the few remaining players whose suits hadn't been powered down for point loss. Then she remembered why she had rushed over from the embassy and hurried into the store area. Kelly breathed a sigh of relief when she entered the noise cancellation field around the counter, but then she saw the bloodied face of the Alt mission leader and she froze.

"Libby!" she subvoced urgently. "We have a medical emergency with Methan. Why did you ping me rather than sending a med bot?"

Rinla noticed the arrival of the ambassador and looked up, a bloody towel in her hand.

211

"Can you get another one of these from that nice clerk?" she asked. "The paint they use just won't come out of his hair."

"Paint?" Kelly sagged in relief and quickly found a fresh towel under the counter to hand the Alt woman. "They never allowed red paintballs when Paul was running the place. Are you sure you're alright, Methan?"

"To be perfectly honest with you, I feel a bit strange," he said, opening one eye to look at the EarthCent ambassador. "I understand that in order to score points in this game one needs to collect paintballs. But somehow we went from catching paintballs in our baskets and shooting them back at inanimate targets to shooting at each other. I suppose it's true that sometimes the other players catch the balls that are shot in their direction, my children demonstrated an innate facility for this, but there were moments when I almost felt like we were struggling for survival."

"But what happened to you? Your head should have been protected by the hood and the face shield."

"I thought that if I just talked to all of the young people, I might persuade them to work together to maximize the opportunity for catches, rather than covering each other in paint. So I took off the hood and the shield, but I'm afraid I wasn't able to make myself understood over the music."

"Does the paint sting in your closed eye? I'm sure it's supposed to be nontoxic for all species."

"My fault, I'm afraid. I put on a miniature over-the-eye recorder to capture the memory for my children, and I forgot it was there when I tried to wipe the paint away. I might have scratched my cornea, but I'm sure it will heal quite nicely on its own."

"I'm taking you to have it checked out by a doctor," Kelly insisted. "We can't have you walking around for the rest of your visit with one eye closed, and what will your people think if we send you home with an eye patch?"

"They'll think he's become a pirate," Rinla said, and to the ambassador's surprise, the two Alts shared a smile. Methan's wife went on to explain. "We took the family to an animated immersive about piracy last night. It's supposed to be the biggest hit on your tunnel network, so I'm sure you must have seen it."

"The one where the animal performers take over the spaceship that's transporting them to a new circus, and then go around the galaxy rescuing everybody?" Kelly fought back the urge to tell the Alts that the production had been financed by an umbrella organization of real pirates working to improve their image. It hadn't escaped EarthCent's attention that the bad guys were all human zookeepers.

"The little squirrel in command was so cute with her tiny eye patch. And the bear that couldn't stop himself from stealing honey!" The Alts shared chuckle at the memory.

"I'm glad to see you're feeling good enough to laugh, but you still have your eye squinted shut," Kelly said testily. "Please let me take you to a doctor. I feel guilty about suggesting that Paul bring you here."

"Very well," Methan said, straightening up on the cot. "Am I presentable enough to appear in public?"

"Almost," Rinla said, folding the towel to get a clean section and taking a final swipe at her husband's face. "We'll have to be careful or you'll start a new fashion trend with the funny colors in your hair."

"I'll ping the station librarian to find out where you are so I can bring him back after we see the doctor," Kelly promised Rinla. "If you ever get the children out of their flying suits, I recommend you ask Paul to bring you to the Wetlands Machine. It's my favorite place in Libbyland."

Methan kept his left eye closed as Kelly led him to the nearest lift tube, which she instructed to bring them to the Stryx emergency med bay. When the doors slid open, they found themselves just a few paces away from the operating table in a room loaded with specialized medical equipment for treating all of the oxygen breathing species that had ever presented at Union Station.

"You!" Kelly said.

"There's always a couple of Humans at the end of every shift," M793qK grumbled. "And for somebody who objected so strongly to wearing a sterilization envelope generator, you show a marked reluctance to part with it."

"I haven't had the time since we got back, and I keep forgetting that I have it on," Kelly admitted, annoyed with herself. "And Methan isn't human. He's the head of the Alt delegation to the tunnel network."

"That's what I get for trusting my multifaceted eyes rather than paying attention to the scanners. I thought he was just a Human with a large head." The Farling approached with his blood draw pistol, which he pressed against the Alt's neck. "That didn't hurt a bit."

"No, it didn't," Methan agreed. "The problem is with my eye. It's just a little scratch on the cornea, but the ambassador insisted."

"Hop on the table and I'll have a look," the beetle instructed his patient. "I'm going to pull up your eyelid and put in an anesthetic drop so you can keep it open without pain." The Alt nodded his assent, and the doctor quickly followed through on his words using a device attached to an articulated metal arm, which he pulled down from an array of accessories above the operating table. "Better?"

"Yes, thank you." Methan peered around the room.

"Close your other eye. How many ambassadors do you see?"

"Just the one," the Alt replied. "But her head seems to be offset on her neck."

"Look up a little higher."

"Now her nose is off center."

"That's what I thought, but I wanted a second opinion," the Farling cracked, rubbing his forelegs together with glee.

"Are you going to do a standup routine or fix his eye!" Kelly practically shouted, stamping her foot at the same time.

"If you damage that sterilization equipment on your ankle you'll have to pay for it," the beetle warned her. "As to the gentleman's eye, I have no objections to carrying out a repair if he is willing to allow me."

"It would be a shame to walk around with monocular vision when we're only here for a brief visit," the Alt replied.

"Look at my left mandible," the beetle commanded, and pulled down a particularly complex-looking piece of equipment that reminded Kelly of her recent visit to the ophthalmologist's office. "Will you be able to keep your eye steady while I operate?"

"Yes, I think so," Methan answered.

"I'm going to count to three, slowly so the Human can keep up with me. One. Two. Three."

Kelly caught herself counting along with the Farling surgeon, and decided on the spot that if he had the gall to show up for another one of Joe's poker games, she was going to spit in his beer. The only saving grace was that the

215

Alt didn't seem to notice the stream of insults, probably because nobody was snarky on their homeworld.

"How does it look?" Methan asked.

"I'll just have to make a tweak to the other side to make sure you don't start favoring the good eye."

"I'm sure when the injury heals my vision will return to its natural balance. I'm fortunate that the damage was to my weak eye."

"Humanoids," the doctor said dismissively. "Only two eyes, but you're ready to settle for just one in good working order. I've restored your damaged eye to its maximum possible efficiency, and if I don't bring the other one up to par, you'll end up not using it." He pushed the rig to the other side of the Alt's head, and then reached out with a pair of limbs to keep the patient's head straight. "All together now. One. Two. Three."

"Did you say you already repaired his eye?" Kelly asked the doctor. "I thought you were just measuring."

"I believe your husband mentioned that Humans have a saying about measuring twice and cutting once, but as you mature as a species, you'll find that it makes more sense to measure and cut at the same time. It eliminates quantum uncertainty."

"Can I stand up now?" Methan asked.

"Just a moment," the Farling said, issuing a silent command to the med bay. Then he pointed to a holographic vision chart which had appeared at the far end of the room. "Tell me the number of fingers held up by the humanoids on the smallest line of the chart you can see."

"Five. One. One. Two. Four. One."

"That's as good as the mechanics of your eyeballs will allow," the doctor said, satisfied with the results of his work. "If you'll change places with the ambassador, I can remove her ankle bracelet, and we'll all be on our way."

Kelly was tempted to stay put for the sake of refusing, but she wanted to get the device off her ankle, so she complied grudgingly. Sitting on the table, she glanced over at the holographic eye chart and found that even by squinting, she could only make out the fingers held up by the figures in the largest row. The Farling looked up from fiddling with the lock on the ankle bracelet and caught her at it.

"Just read off the fingers in the highest row you can manage," he instructed her.

"Five. One. One. Two. Four. One," Kelly recited from memory.

"Come now. Do you really think I didn't change the test while you were swapping places?"

"You're bluffing," the ambassador guessed.

Methan, who hadn't stopped peering at different points in the room with a childish look of wonder since he rose from the table, inspected the eye chart again.

"Four. Six. Six. One. Six. Six," he read off. "Must have drafted a bunch of those Drazen fellows to pose for the illustration."

"If you come by my shop, I'll fix those eyes up for you," the Farling told the ambassador, unsnapping the ankle bracelet and straightening up.

"My vision has never been so good, and I didn't feel a thing," Methan encouraged her. "Mashing that miniature camera into my eye turned out to be a tremendous bit of luck. Thank you, Doctor."

"Why can't you just fix my eyes here?" Kelly asked suspiciously.

"My shift is almost up and med bay usage is allocated by the Stryx. Of course, if you ask the station manager for special treatment…"

"No. I'll think about it," Kelly said, hating herself for the fact that she was even considering letting the Farling fix her eyes. Besides, she had just paid thirty creds for new prescription reading glasses, though she avoided letting anybody outside of the family and Dring see her wearing them. "How much would it cost?"

"Ten creds an eye," the beetle offered, which made her feel even worse. "And I'd waive the charge if you'd give me permission to extract a few of those interesting microbes from your gut. I have a theory that if I combined enough genetic material from your microbiome, I could come up with a new species at least as advanced as Humans."

"You can harvest microbes from my gut," the Alt offered.

"I'll let you know if I want to take you up on the offer after I get back to my shop and run a sequence from your blood sample. I can see from the med bay scanners that both your diet and digestive system are superior to the ambassador's, so you aren't as dependent on symbiotic relationships with your intestinal community."

"How can you make comparisons about our digestive systems when we're different species eating different things?" Kelly objected.

"You and your diets are more compatible than you realize. If I were going by outward appearances, I'd put you at two-thousandth cousins, or thereabouts."

Kelly's implant pinged with an incoming message from Paul, so she pointed at her ear to be polite and listened to his update. It turned out that Bork had told Antha about the medieval castle where the Drazen had participated in a battle reenactment. Rinla was curious to see if there were parallels between human and Alt history, so they were heading there for lunch.

"Let's go," she said to Methan. "Your family is on their way to visit the last Libbyland attraction that Paul helped build before he went into the used spaceship business. It's a sort of a generic reconstruction of a castle from around a thousand years ago."

"Castle?" the Alt inquired.

"A giant pile of stones from which one group of Humans could dominate another group by dropping things on them from a height," the doctor explained. "The Grenouthians produced an excellent documentary on the subject in which they examined whether the walls were intended to keep people in or out."

"What was the final determination?"

"The scientists on the panel couldn't agree on why anybody would want to live in a cold and drafty building to start with, but the whole point became moot when Humans developed siege engines that could batter down the walls."

"It all sounds very violent," Methan said.

"Most humanoids go through a phase of bashing each other on the heads with hard objects, and a surprising number of them look back on such times with great sentimentality," the Farling explained. "From what I read off the chart, your species is an exception."

"He has a chart?" Kelly asked skeptically.

"The Stryx provide background data for all patients referred to the med bay. And in answer to your next question, no, you can't see it."

"That wasn't my next question," Kelly lied, but she couldn't think of another one to substitute.

Nineteen

"Dorothy's home," Vivian announced, stepping back and lowering her foil.

"You think I'm falling for that old trick?" Samuel replied scornfully. He remained on his guard, not giving in to the temptation to look over his shoulder, but the girl proceeded to remove her protective face shield. "You're serious?"

"I'm flattered that you're so focused on me, but you really should learn to keep an eye on your surroundings. I just completed the InstaSitter training course, and they stressed that most accidents happen when the sitter is paying too much attention to the client to notice that the cat has fallen into the fish tank."

"You're talking about situational awareness," the boy said, removing his own mask. "It's part of the EarthCent Intelligence training."

"I'll bet they stole it from us. Incoming," she warned suddenly, going into a protective crouch.

"What?" Samuel spun towards the parking area and registered the fact that Kevin's ship had in fact arrived and the ramp was already descending. Then a fast-moving blur coming in from an oblique angle tore his mask out of his hand and streaked away across the hold. "Alexander!" he shouted after the dog. "Bring that back!"

"Look, Beowulf is already chasing him. I'll bet Alex just took it to get his dad's attention."

"We'd better go see if Dorothy and Kevin need help with anything. I'll come back for our stuff later." Samuel piled his remaining gear on the unused scorer's table, and Vivian followed suit. Then the two teens headed for the recently arrived ship.

"I can't believe we're already back," Dorothy said, looking out at Mac's Bones from the top of the ramp. "It feels like we left yesterday."

"Yesterday you were complaining that we'd been in the tunnel forever," Kevin reminded her.

"What did I tell you about repeating things I say back to me? And don't forget that our companionship contract stipulated that I get half of the profits for this trip."

"Why do you think I kept asking you to go over the books?"

"I'll have Paul do that for me. Or Dad. Or Jeeves. Or anyone. How'd we do?"

"Pretty average until Ailia's business agent bought all the trade goods that fit under their tech ban and overpaid with cash."

"Where did you put the gifts she gave us for the family?"

"Stow. I stowed the gifts in the set of lockers right next to the ramp so they would be easy to get at."

"Here comes Samuel. He must be in a hurry to see what Ailia sent him." Dorothy opened the locker with a palm swipe and began pulling out the presents. "I'll bet you that Aisha breaks down and cries when she sees this tapestry that the princess wove for her."

"It's the cylinder Ailia sent for Vivian that I'm curious about, but remember not to mention it to Sam."

"What's in the metal chest?"

"Dog toys for Beowulf. She had the blacksmith solder it closed so that Alexander wouldn't steal them. Hey, Sam. Hello, Vivian. How's university treating you?"

"A lot of work," the boy replied.

"Ailia said that she's told you to drop the dual major in Vergallian Studies a dozen times, but you won't listen," Dorothy said. "It's not like you could ever get a space engineering job on a tech-ban world."

"A man needs something to think about when he's walking behind a plow."

"That's why I don't pester him about it," Vivian spoke up, and proceeded to repurpose Samuel's reply. "A space engineer needs something to dream about or he'll turn into a machine. Besides, learning about the most populous humanoid culture on the tunnel network can only help us down the road."

"This one is for you, Sam," Kevin continued, handing over a garment bag. "There's a box here for your family as well, Vivian."

"She sent a gift for everybody she knew on Union Station," Dorothy added. "There's a sculpture for Dring, presents for all the cast members who were on 'Let's Make Friends' with her, and she even gave us something for Jeeves. Where is everybody, anyway? I asked Libby to ping the folks when we came out of the tunnel."

"They're all inside," Samuel said, adding the thin package for Jeeves to the pile of gifts for the McAllister household.

"A surprise party, huh?" Dorothy asked, trying to sound bored by the idea. "I told mom not to do anything special."

"She's just having another work meeting. There's a new species that's practically human and everybody's pretty excited about them. I think tonight's the official press conference before the Alt delegation returns home and puts the tunnel network to a vote or something."

Inside the ice harvester, the ambassador was directing Daniel and Thomas in handing boxes of books out of Dorothy's room, even while she gathered up clothes that were piled on the girl's bed.

"She wasn't supposed to be back until next week," Kelly apologized. "It's just that her room makes such a convenient staging area that I couldn't help taking advantage to reorganize some things."

"It's not like you rented it out," Thomas reassured her. "Chance and I are happy to help. We were already on our way to the training camp to work on a new hologram when Clive pinged about the meeting."

"Where did you want these?" Blythe called from the living room.

"Just stack the books in front of the shelves for now, and throw the dirty clothes on the floor of the laundry room. I can't believe how I let things get so backed up, but this is the last batch. I'll just change her sheets and I'll be right out."

"Sorry we're late," Lynx said, entering the ice harvester with Woojin and the baby. "Are you guys moving or something?"

"Covering up is more like it." Joe set down the box of books he was carrying and pointed at the baby. "Is she cleared for high level intelligence?"

"She's smarter than her father, if that's what you mean," Lynx shot back. "Em. Who's a big worrywart?"

"Dada!"

"And do you swear to uphold the values of EarthCent and the cause of humanity?" Blythe adlibbed from the EarthCent Intelligence oath.

"Mama?"

"Close enough," Lynx said, giving Em a kiss. "Where do you get all the new books from, anyway? They must have cost a fortune."

"Kelly's mom goes to estate sales and sends us a few more in every diplomatic pouch," Joe replied, while moving a couple of carbon fiber chairs from the dining room table into the living room area. "They add up pretty fast."

"All right. If everybody will grab a seat, we can get started," Clive announced. "I'm sorry for the short notice, but I received an intelligence update from our Drazen friends an hour ago that agrees with our own assessment. The Vergallians plan to offer the Alts a place in their empire."

"The Alts will never go for it," Daniel predicted, settling onto the couch. "It's all about family with them. Shaina and I have been taking groups from their delegation around the Shuk, and when they found out that Shaina's father owns Kitchen Kitsch, they insisted on buying things from him just to honor the connection. It drove Peter nuts because they don't know how to haggle. It was pretty funny watching him drive a hard bargain with himself in hopes of teaching the Alts how a real market works."

"Sounds to me like they were employing a successful tactic," Blythe said.

"And I'm not sure I see the connection between buying kitchen gadgets and rejecting the Vergallian offer," Clive added.

"The whole concept of making deals seems to have escaped the Alts. They expect everybody to function like a fairy-tale family with shared goals, which hardly describes the Vergallians. None of the other species understand how

224

the Alts were able to develop an advanced technological society without a hierarchical government. It's not normal for humanoids."

"They are incredibly cooperative," Lynx said. "At first I thought it's just that they have a highly developed sense of empathy, but talking to them, they have no tradition of conflict at all."

"Every one of the Alts I've interviewed with would get top scores on our InstaSitter test," Blythe contributed. "But we're worried they might accept the Vergallian offer without really understanding what it means. Abeva is smart enough to make it look like an invitation to join a larger family, and if they're as susceptible to pheromones as we are, she could try to influence Methan to champion their proposal."

"I already warned him about that," Daniel said. "What worries me is that they've been putting off making any deals with business groups from my sovereign human communities. I can understand being cautious, but the Alts all take the line that they can't make any commitments before putting the matter before everybody back home. Do they intend to decide every little thing with some kind of planetary vote?"

Kelly set a tray of snacks on the coffee table and perched on the edge of her Love-U massaging recliner. "What puzzles me is why their youngest children get upset whenever one of us enters the room. You'd think that they would be more comfortable with adults who look like their parents, but one of their little girls ran to hide behind Ambassador Crute when I asked her name."

"I don't believe they've attempted to conceal anything from us," Thomas said. "As near as I can tell, they aren't capable of even minor deceptions."

"I don't suspect Methan, I suspect the Stryx," Kelly insisted stubbornly. "I can always tell when they're trying to get away with something."

"I feel like I've been operating as a real cultural attaché for the first time," Lynx said. "Everything about the Alts fascinates me, and their traditions echo our own in funny ways. It's like we started out on the same road, but took different turns at some point. Did you know why all of their young women have that long braid?"

"Hadn't noticed," Clive admitted.

"It's for courting. The young man grabs the girl's braid in one hand..."

"Neanderthals!" the ambassador interrupted.

"No, it's really very sweet," Lynx protested. "It's a substitute for grooming since they don't have bugs in their hair."

"They're Neanderthals," Kelly reiterated, her voice rising in pitch. "Our Neanderthals. The Stryx took them from Earth and gave them their own planet."

There was a brief moment of stunned silence, and then Clive asked, "Is this just a gut feeling, or do you have evidence? I thought that Neanderthals died out tens of thousands of years ago."

"I'm sure of it," Kelly insisted. "That's why the Farling said we could be two-thousandth cousins. I thought he was just making fun of me, but it all fits together. Haven't you noticed that when you talk with Alts about our respective worlds we always understand each other? There aren't any of those awkward translations, like, 'an eight-legged animal with orange stripes on blue fur.' I should have known there was something fishy when Methan said that their translation devices were designed for communicating with dogs and dolphins. Everybody has dogs, but dolphins?"

"Squirrels!" Lynx exclaimed. "All of the Alts loved that propaganda immersive the pirates produced, and two different women told me that the squirrel with the eyepatch reminded them of the ones that raid their bird-feeders back home."

"The Farling took a blood sample," Kelly recalled suddenly. "Somebody has to go and talk to him."

"I'll do it," Lynx volunteered. "I was going to bring Em by to see him anyway. She loves visiting her Uncle Beetle."

"And I'm going to talk to Stryx Wylx," Kelly said. "Maybe I can finally get something out of her."

"Hold on a minute," Chance said. "I know that history isn't my strong suit, but why would the Stryx take the Neanderthals from Earth tens of thousands of years ago and move them to a hidden planet?"

"Might have been that the end of the Ice Ages was doing them in and the Stryx didn't want to see them die out," Joe suggested.

"Shouldn't they all have protruding foreheads and be covered with hair if they're Neanderthals?" Woojin asked.

"Who knows how they would change over a few thousand generations on a new world without any competition," Kelly said. "I listened to a Dollnick salesman explaining climate control to the Alts at the exposition, but apparently they've never given the weather a thought because it's always mild on their world."

"I think it would be best to put off checking with the beetle until the Alts have gone," Clive cautioned. "I can just imagine what the other species would make of this if it leaks out. The press conference is just over an hour away, and if Kelly's right, I wouldn't be surprised if the Stryx originally moved them because our ancestors were killing them off."

"Too late for that," Bork said from the door. "Sorry to show up unannounced, but I couldn't reach you, so I thought I'd try dropping in."

"My fault," Joe said, getting up and going over to an antique radio cabinet where he flipped a switch. "I turned on our electronic countermeasures out of habit."

"How much did you hear, Bork?" Kelly asked.

"Just what Clive said. It was enough to tell me that you've already figured out what I just learned from our own intelligence people."

"You ran genetic tests on us without saying anything?"

"Of course not, Ambassador," Bork replied with dignity. "We spied on the Hortens who ran genetic tests on the Alts and compared them to samples they no doubt took from your people decades ago. Given your similarity to the Alts and your ability to eat most of the same foods, I'm positive that the Vergallians will have done the same by now, but we haven't been able to crack their codes."

"And the Hortens say that we're definitely from the same world?" Clive asked.

"Their test results indicate that over ninety-nine percent of your nucleotide sequences are identical to those of the Alts, if you can trust the scientists of a species that accidentally altered its own genome. And not only do you share a common ancestor in the distant past, but some of your more recent forbearers interbred not too long before the Stryx moved the Alts to their own world."

"Was there anything else in the Horten intercept that you can share?"

"Nothing important," Bork said, looking suddenly uncomfortable. "I'd better get going if I'm going to be in time for the press conference."

Kelly moved quickly to cut off the Drazen ambassador's exit. "They compared us to each other, didn't they?"

"You came out very well by some measures. Despite the Alt's superior technology, the Hortens dismissed them as having no potential for becoming military allies."

"Come on, Bork. You know we're going to hear it sooner or later, so you may as well tell us now."

"Well, the report did go on a bit about just how nice the Alts are. And there might have been a little speculation about why the Stryx felt compelled to move them off of Earth in the first place."

"I knew it. I'll bet the Hortens are saying that the Stryx saved the Alts from us."

"The Hortens also believe that the Stryx saved you from the Vergallians," Bork pointed out. "They never bought into the whole economic apocalypse argument, even though your situation was clearly in dire straits. Now I really do have to run because it takes forever to get into my fancy dress uniform. Welcome home, Dorothy," he added, as the girl entered the ice harvester.

"Thank you, Ambassador. Dressing up for something?"

"Big press conference," Bork said, and leaned in close to Dorothy to whisper, "Your mother was a bit underdressed at the last event, if you take my meaning." Then he headed down the ramp just in time to avoid being trapped by Kevin, Samuel and Vivian, all of whom were burdened by boxes.

"So, when is this press conference?" Dorothy asked, looking around at the gathered EarthCent staff. "Are we the hosts?"

229

"The Alts are the hosts, though the Stryx are paying," Blythe told her. "I suppose the rest of us should be leaving so you have time to get ready, Ambassador. There's nothing we can do about the Alts being Neanderthals at this point, so we'll have to play it by ear."

The others took Blythe's cue and followed the Oxfords out, leaving the McAllister family and Kevin a chance to catch up. Instead, Dorothy overrode her mother's ineffectual protests and herded her into the bedroom to don a formal gown. "And don't you dare come out in flats," the girl admonished her mother.

Joe joined his wife a few minutes later looking sheepish. "I've been instructed to wear one of those jackets Dorothy got me. Do you remember how to tie a tie?"

"Ask Dorothy," Kelly replied, strapping on high heeled shoes for the first time in over a year. "I've got to practice walking."

"What do you really make of the Stryx evacuating the Neanderthals, Kel?" Joe asked after donning his dressjacket. He rolled up a tie and put it in his pocket.

"I tried pinging Libby a few times, but she says the Alts are Wylx's project, and then she clams up."

"So what does Wylx say?"

"She puts me off by asking if I have any more advice for raising Spinner. I never thought a Stryx could be so infuriating."

"My ears are burning," Jeeves declared, floating past the bedroom door.

"I wasn't talking about you," Kelly replied in irritation. "Are you here to gloat about how the human relatives we thought were extinct and whose very name came to mean 'primitive' ended up being peaceful geniuses who beat us to developing their own faster-than-light-drive?"

"I hadn't thought of it that way, though you make a compelling argument. I was invited by Samuel to pick up a package that Ailia sent me, and I was going to stop in anyway because Dorothy is ignoring my pings."

"What did my daughter do now?" Joe asked, prepared to be amused at the Stryx's expense.

"She committed me to a large expenditure on unproven heel technology," Jeeves replied. "The bills from Chintoo are already mounting up."

"Don't try to change the subject," Kelly said. "Bork told us that the Hortens never bought the argument that the Stryx opened Earth because of our economic problems. They think you did it to keep us from getting absorbed into the Vergallian Empire."

"I wasn't even alive yet, you know."

"Don't give me that. Libby puts me off on Wylx and Wylx—it doesn't matter. I'm asking you straight out why the Stryx find Earth so interesting."

"Hey, Jeeves," Samuel said, emerging from his own room. He handed over the package that Kevin had given him. "Ailia sent this for you."

"Just in time," the Stryx replied, grabbing it with his pincer. "I'd love to stay and chat, Ambassador, but I have to be in court on a serious matter. Please tell Dorothy that we're having an urgent meeting at our offices in one hour."

"Coward," Kelly yelled after him.

Twenty

"If you're too tired after coming through the tunnel, we could do this another time," Shaina offered.

"I'm wide awake," Dorothy replied, and gave Kevin's shoulder a shake. "He's the sleepy one."

"If you're sure," Brinda said. "I've been waiting to ask if you actually tried on any shoes that used the Verlock heels."

"The prototype pair the inventor brought to Chintoo was designed for his wife. I would have had to put on combat boots first or my feet would have been swimming around in them."

"The Verlock showed a holo of his wife walking through an obstacle course in the heels," Kevin explained tiredly. "He even poured out a bag of marbles on the floor to demonstrate the gyroscopic correction feature."

"I'm sure his wife must have loved that," Shaina said. "Jeeves disappeared for a couple of days after Ug contacted us, and he brought back some of the samples that the inventor left behind on Chintoo. The technology is impressive, but we aren't sure how it will work in practice. Think about when you're dancing with a partner and he dips you. What if the heels try to keep you upright?"

"That's just programming," the girl said dismissively. "How hard can it be to tell the difference between a dance move and a loss of balance?"

"That depends on who's dancing," Flazint said. "I'm looking forward to trying the shoes myself, and I might have gotten into the Verlock pair with a just little padding, but imagine if you put them on Chance."

"Chance would never buy them because she's got built-in gyroscopes already. And we don't have to include all three of the advanced features in every pair. Just the memory-metal adjustable height will let us compete with the 'S' design that the Vergallians sell for big creds."

"What was the third feature?" Affie asked.

"A dynamically adjusted heel-tip area to prevent the Verlock women from poking holes in the floor. But it's not about the wearer's weight, it's about the interaction at the surface. The tip of the heel will flatten out so that you or I could walk on grass or sand without taking off our shoes."

"I like walking in grass and sand barefoot," Flazint protested.

"Barefoot is okay if you don't mind being short."

"We really think that they have great potential, Dorothy, and we've already discussed rolling out the features in stages," Shaina said. "Combining them in different ways will give us seven different models, which means seven price points. The easiest feature for manufacturing is the memory-metal height adjustment, and Ug has already started on an initial order."

"I thought he said it would take like five months."

"That was for the full-featured heel. The other advantage to breaking the development into stages is that it spreads out the cost for us."

"You mean for Jeeves. Where is he, anyway?"

"Right here," the Stryx said, floating through the doorway. "I was busy fulfilling my duties under the powers vested in me by, well, by being me."

"What could be more important than new heel technology?"

"You do know that your mother is attending a press conference for the departing Alt mission as we speak."

"So what's your point?"

"I wish you luck in your marriage," Jeeves said to Kevin.

"Oh, so now you're saying I'm difficult?" Dorothy demanded.

"No, I'm offering my con—is it my imagination or is your metabolism running fast?" The Stryx moved closer to Dorothy, who tried to look nonchalant and failed. "Do I detect a banned Farling substance in your bloodstream?"

"It's a prescription for Zero-G sickness. We just got out of the tunnel a couple of hours ago." Then her mind caught up with the Stryx's previous sentence, and she demanded, "Were you about to offer Kevin condolences on being my boyfriend?"

"No, I was about to offer you both my congratulations. But first, tell me the truth. Were you using that drug when you told Ug to make the deal for the heels?"

"The beetle assured me that he took out the addictive part and whatever made it illegal," Kevin interjected in Dorothy's defense. "Besides, I started cutting the patches in half after the first time she got, uh, overly energized."

"Try cutting them in quarters on the next trip," Brinda suggested.

Dorothy shushed the other humans and grabbed onto the Stryx's pincer so he couldn't float away. "What congratulations?"

"On your marriage," Jeeves said calmly.

"WHAT MARRIAGE?"

"The one you entered into by fulfilling the terms of your Frunge contract."

"Congratulations!" Flazint shouted. "When were you going to tell us?"

"I don't have a clue what Jeeves is talking about," Dorothy spluttered, letting go of the pincer and turning to her boyfriend. "Do you, Kevin?"

"I'm too tired to follow all of this. Can you dumb it down for me, Jeeves?"

"Perhaps this will jog your memories," the Stryx said, producing a document. "This is a copy, so there's no point in trying to destroy it. I've already deposited the original affidavit with the Frunge Honor Court."

"I can't read this," Dorothy objected. "What is it?"

"It's in Frunge," Flazint said, taking it up and beginning to read. "I, Ailia, heir to the throne of Avidiya, daughter of Atuba, granddaughter of Avilia, great-granddaughter of Aagra, do solemnly witness the fulfillment of a Frunge companionship contract engraved in the names of Kevin Crick and Dorothy McAllister of Union Station. They exchanged their vows in the presence of myself and the Cayl hound Alexander in the private dining room of the Mercenary Tavern in the ninth year of the reign of Royal Protector Baylit, my half-sister." The Frunge girl turned to Dorothy, her cheeks wet with tears. "You finally did it. You're married."

"What vows? We didn't exchange any vows that I know of!"

"Are you sure? The contract uses the standard formula. If you said, 'I want to marry Kevin,' and he said, 'I want to marry Dorothy,' in front of two witnesses, then it's a done deal."

"I kind of remember that now," Kevin said, coming wide awake. "So we're really married?"

"It doesn't count because Alexander is underage," Dorothy objected desperately.

"I hate to be the one to point this out, but Vergallian royals count double as witnesses," Affie told her. "That's why the queens are always saying stuff like, 'We are not amused,' in dramas."

"But this is even worse than getting married by a fake Elvis!" Dorothy wailed. "Mom is never going to let me live it down. Listen, none of you can tell anybody. We'll have a real wedding as soon as I can make a dress."

"Of course you will," Flazint cooed to comfort the distraught girl. "The contract is just a legal thing. Everybody still has weddings."

"The delay will give you time to go through rehab for your Zero-G drug addiction," Jeeves suggested. Dorothy took a swing at his metal casing and would have broken her knuckles if the Stryx hadn't retreated at supersonic speed.

A minute later, Jeeves eased his way into the ballroom of the Camelot hotel/casino, where the Alt press conference was just getting under way.

"Bob Steelforth, Galactic Free Press. Will you be recommending that your people vote in favor of joining the tunnel network?"

"Thank you for the question," Methan responded politely. "First let me say that my colleagues and my family have asked me to speak for them today. Unfortunately, I'm afraid that none of us are familiar with this concept of 'voting' that we're suddenly hearing so much about."

"It's another term for coming to a collective decision, sort of," the reporter tried to explain. "Were you chosen as the delegation leader through an election? I mean, a vote? I mean, you know what I mean."

"We discussed the options and everybody thought it best that we speak with one voice." Methan seemed to feel he had answered the question adequately because he pointed at a Vergallian reporter. "Yes?"

"Imperial Times," the correspondent declared, without bothering to give his name. "Now that you'll be joining the Vergallian Empire, will you be seeking royal status for any of your own people, or will you petition the high council to have queens assigned to your worlds?"

"Thank you for the question," Methan said, ignoring the sudden chatter from the diplomats and reporters present. "It's true that your lovely ambassador has official-ly invited us to join the Vergallian Empire, and my people will take it under consideration along with the tunnel network tender."

"Do you seriously mean that your people would risk offending the largest empire on the tunnel network by refusing?" the reporter demanded.

"Next question," Methan said, sounding like an old pro at politics and pointing at a Horten.

"Legal Informer. Will you seek the return of your for-mer property on Earth?" the alien correspondent asked.

"Stryx Wylx has explained that our population was lim-ited to a relatively small number of hunter-gatherer clans when she removed us from our original home. I don't know what territorial claims our ancestors may have made, but I believe I speak for all of my people in saying that bygones are bygones and we're perfectly happy with our current situation."

"How about trademark infringement?" a Thark correspondent inquired, without waiting to be called on. "You're practically the same species."

"I'm not sure I understand the question."

"They're running around the galaxy opening up businesses like 'Human this' and 'Human that' as if they owned the trademark. I happen to know an excellent intellectual property attorney."

"Ah, a semantics issue. It's not my field of expertise." Methan turned to the group of Alts standing behind him, but nobody seemed inclined to take up the legal question. "I don't see a problem with our distant relations from Earth using their name for themselves for commercial purposes."

"Is it true that Stryx Wylx intervened to prevent the Humans from killing you off?" a Grenouthian reporter demanded.

"Please watch your language, there may be children listening," Methan scolded the reporter. He offered a silent thanks to his wife for talking him into accepting free InstaSitter babysitting for all of the young ones during the press conference. "I have no information that any violence was offered to our ancestors by the Humans. In fact, the genetic analysis provided by my Farling physician suggests that we are more them than they are us, if you want to talk percentages. He speculated that the admixture is based on the relative sizes of our founding populations."

"Kristine, Children's News Network," a teenage girl announced herself. "Will you be visiting Earth anytime soon?"

"We would like very much to visit your planet, but due to our similarity at the cellular level, the life sciences team is concerned about the possibility of our contracting diseases to which we have no immunity. My Farling physician has offered a solution, but I'm not sure we can afford it, at least for large numbers of us."

"We've had reports that your children are instinctively frightened by Humans," a different Grenouthian reporter called out. "Isn't that proof that you were removed from Earth for your own safety?"

"I don't see any advantage to pursuing that line of questioning," Methan responded. "Stryx Wylx hasn't given her reason for removing us, nor will she confirm or deny transplanting other branches of our common family tree to as-of-yet hidden worlds. Perhaps we were the aggressors and the meek were left to inherit the Earth."

"Baloney," the bunny practically spat. "You wouldn't say that if you'd watched any of our documentaries."

"What about it?" Kelly muttered to Dring, who had accompanied the McAllisters to the press conference, where they stood with the other ambassadors and their spouses. "Do you know anything about this that you aren't saying?"

"It's all very recent history to me, if you can even call it such," the Maker whispered. "I haven't heard a specific date cited, but I was on the other side of the galaxy for most of the last few million years."

"Michael, Children's News Network. When can we expect a decision on your joining the tunnel network or the Vergallian Empire?"

"Ah, yes. All of our people will gather to discuss these offers in their own families, though of course some of the younger children will need time to mature before they can participate in a meaningful manner. The offer was extended to all living Alts, and it wouldn't be fair for those of us who happen to be older to make such a momentous decision that would be nearly impossible to reverse at a later date."

"Follow-up question," Michael called politely. "Are you talking about a number of years?"

"Yes, precisely," Methan said. The noise level in the room swelled as everybody began talking at once, and the Alt representative inclined his head to his wife, who whispered in his ear. "I should add that we will first consider the issue of trade with other species, starting with the import of Frunge bicycles."

Then a Verlock asked a question about the mathematical system the Alts had employed in developing their model of the universe, and Methan launched into an enthusiastic explanation. The other correspondents began slipping out of the room to file reports, and some of the alien diplomats and their spouses started looking around for chairs.

"I've never heard of the Stryx choosing a group of sentients from a viable world and moving them to their own planet," Kelly said to Dring in what was now a general murmur of conversation. "They may have interfered in the development of humanoid species by diddling with our genes, but playing nursemaid to a bunch of hunter-gatherers?"

"It's possible that the Stryx were acting on assumptions they made about our history," Dring admitted quietly. "Don't forget that their scientific ability surpassed our own soon after we created them, and they may have tracked our origin to your Earth. I don't remember our homeworld, and neither do my brothers, but some of us speculate that we chose to forget in order to lessen the trauma of a great disaster."

"But I guessed that fifteen years ago!" Kelly cried, drawing attention from the other ambassadors, who preferred anything over Methan's verbal recitation of a mathematical proof. "Joe. Didn't I say that the Maker's lost world was Earth the first time Dring shifted into a dragon?"

"Are you saying that the Stryx view you and the Alts as family?" the Grenouthian ambassador demanded loudly. The room fell silent, and everybody waited for the EarthCent ambassador's response.

"No, I—how should I know what the Stryx are thinking?" Kelly spotted Jeeves floating at the back of the room and pointed at him like she was making an accusation. "Have you been treating us special all along because you think that the Makers started out on Earth?"

"I like to think of all sentient beings as my family," Jeeves replied evasively, and then employed one of his favorite tactics from his soon-to-be-published manual on diplomatic conversation changers. "Did you know that Dorothy is married?"

"I think that Aunt Kelly may have a cavity in her third molar on the upper right," Vivian observed, as the Grenouthian cameraman zoomed in on the gaping mouth of the EarthCent ambassador.

Blythe waved the hologram of the press conference out of existence as a stunned Kelly began accepting congratulations from her alien friends, and everyone else present took the opportunity to flee, leaving the Verlock taking mathematical notes as Methan droned on.

"How does it feel to witness history?" Blythe asked the twins.

241

"I'd rather make history," Jonah replied seriously. "I'm taking the dog for a walk. Want to come, Viv?"

"I've got homework to finish," his sister replied, eliciting groans from the whole family, including the dog. "What? You have something against higher education?"

"I had a look at the senior year electives for your Dynastic Studies major," Clive said. "There's a course on consolidating your power that looked an awful lot like a euphemism for eliminating competing family members."

"Don't worry, Dad," Vivian said, leaning over and planting a kiss on the top of his head as she passed behind the couch. "I don't see any of you as competition."

"When I figure out what that means, young lady, you may be in trouble."

"So what was in that scroll tube that Princess Ailia sent you?" Blythe asked her daughter.

"A title. It's sort of a friendly joke on her part since it doesn't have any legal validity for humans."

"Countess Vivian, I presume," her father said in a mock serious voice. "You know I have ample experience as a royal bodyguard."

"I'll keep it in mind when I'm consolidating my power," the girl shot back. Then she stuck out her tongue at him and fled to her room. There she took up the metal tube Ailia had sent her and carefully removed the rolled-up parchment, laying it face down. On the back was a line with a few words printed in Vergallian and a signature followed by a royal seal. Vivian got out her calligraphy supplies and carefully wrote her own name below Ailia's signature. Then she blew gently on the Verlock ink, the warmth from her breath drying it immediately.

"Well, I guess that's that," she said out loud, turning over the parchment and admiring the picture. "All I need now is a frame and a mat with a wide border."

The watercolor and ink drawing of Samuel at age seven, sitting on the ramp of the ice harvester next to Beowulf and looking impatient, bore witness to the fact that the princess was blessed with photographic recall. On a blank space of the ice-harvester hull, in an area that Ailia must have known could easily be concealed by framing, the Vergallian girl had printed in English:

Certificate of Title. New owner must sign back to complete transfer.

EarthCent Ambassador Series:

About the Author

E. M. Foner lives in Northampton, MA with an imaginary German Shepherd who's been trained to bite bankers. The author welcomes reader comments at e_foner@yahoo.com.

Other books by the author:

Meghan's Dragon

Turing Test

Lightning Source UK Ltd.
Milton Keynes UK
UKHW03f150300318
320279UK00001B/297/P